A

MILLION MILES

FROM HOME

A
MILLION MILES
FROM HOME

MIKE DELLOSSO

FIREFLY
SOUTHERN FICTION
LIGHTHOUSE PUBLISHING OF THE CAROLINAS

A MILLION MILES FROM HOME BY MIKE DELLOSSO
Published by Firefly Southern Fiction
an imprint of Lighthouse Publishing of the Carolinas
2333 Barton Oaks Dr., Raleigh, NC 27614

ISBN: 978-1-946016-49-2
Copyright © 2018 by Mike Dellosso
Cover design by Elaina Lee
Interior design by AtriTeX Technologies P Ltd

Available in print from your local bookstore, online, or from the publisher at: lpcbooks.com

For more information on this book and the author visit: michaelkingbooks. wordpress.com

Brought to you by the creative team at Lighthouse Publishing of the Carolinas: Eva Marie Everson, Jessica R. Everson, Shonda Savage

Library of Congress Cataloging-in-Publication Data

Dellosso, Mike

A Million Miles From Home / Mike Dellosso 1st ed.

Printed in the United States of America

Praise for *A MILLION MILES FROM HOME*

In a style that reminds me of Pat Conroy, Mike Delloso takes his readers on a journey of familial joys and sorrows ... of love and loss ... of life and death ... and of the redemption that only comes from reaching into the past to live in the present and, in turn, to embrace the future.

~**Eva Marie Everson**
CBA Bestselling, Award-winning Author
The One True Love of Alice-Ann

While exploring a topic that other authors might shy away from, Mike Dellosso shines. In *A Million Miles from Home*, he handles the story of a young mother's death with his characteristic sensitivity and grace. Offering an honest portrayal of loss and grief, he skillfully walks the reader through the bereaved husband and daughter's journey toward hope and healing. An uplifting read and immensely satisfying.

~**Ann Tatlock**
Novelist, Editor, and Children's Book Author

ACKNOWLEDGMENTS

THIS IS THE PART where I get to reveal the group of folks "behind the curtain" who make writing and publishing a book possible.

My family comes first. My wife and daughters are such an inspiration to me and always play a role in my books. Every time I write about a wife or mother I draw from my wife. Every time I write about a young girl or woman I draw from my daughters. I'm fortunate to live with such strong, beautiful (inside and out) women who inspire me and push me. Because of the content of this book there were lots of emotions to work through during the writing and editing. I hope and pray those emotions only ever live in my imagination.

My editors at Lighthouse Publishing of the Carolinas. Eva Marie Everson for taking a chance on this story. Jessica Everson for her editing advice and suggestions. Both are wonderful at what they do and more wonderful at who they are.

Dennis Martin offered advice about farming and Dr. Kyle Messick gave insight into some of the injury-related aspects in the story.

My readers . . . without you there would be no books. It would just be me talking to myself (which I do a lot anyway). Thank you for sticking with me, supporting me, encouraging me, praying for me.

Lastly (but not lastly), I want to thank my God for giving me an active imagination and a love for storytelling. I hope I never tarnish His name.

For Jen, who I can't imagine doing life without.

CHAPTER 1

I FELL IN LOVE WITH Annie Fleming when I was thirteen.

We were neighbors. Had been since we were in kindergarten and her family moved to Boomer, North Carolina from Detroit. Her daddy had been transferred there. Some new management position at the local bookbinding plant that apparently needed a big city goon to fill it. Annie's daddy beat her on a regular basis. The first time I met her she was hiding in my tree house. At six years old I had no idea what it meant to be beat by your father. My dad was a drunk but he wasn't a violent one. He'd holler and occasionally toss a toaster or dinner plate across the kitchen, but he never once laid a hand on either me or my mother. It just wasn't his style.

When we were thirteen I found Annie again in my tree house. She'd climbed up there after another thumping from her daddy. Her right eye was a little puffy and she had a nasty blue-and-green bruise on her left arm, just above the elbow. She usually did a pretty good job of hiding the bruises but didn't care if I saw them. I was the only one who knew of her secret, of the pain she hid from the rest of the world. I didn't know if her momma was aware of what went on in that home of hers. I figured she was either as dumb and blind as an earthworm and had no clue, or she knew very well what was going on and chose to look away and pretend she didn't. Either way, I hated both of Annie's parents.

That evening, I climbed up into my tree house after dinner and found Annie sitting there in the corner, both knees pulled to her chest, her hair matted and frizzed, her cheeks stained with tears. I walked over and sat next to her, touched the bruise on her arm.

"Does it hurt?"

She shook her head. Annie always shook her head when I asked if her bruises hurt.

Pulling my knees up, I reached for a baseball card on the floor beside me. It was a 1975 George Brett. Kansas City Royals. Holding the card between my thumbs and index fingers I tore it in half, then in quarters.

"I hate him." And I wasn't talking about George Brett. I'd never told Annie how I felt about her daddy. Part of me wanted to reach out and take those words back as soon as they left my mouth and part of me wanted them to hang out there, to float all the way down the tree and across the yard and into the Fleming living room where Annie's father was no doubt perched in front of the TV, beer in hand. I wanted him to know I hated him.

"Don't," she said and her voice cracked. "Hate never solved anyone's problem."

"Killing did. I want to kill him."

Annie turned and shoved me in the arm. Tears poured from her eyes again. "Don't you dare say that, Benjamin Flurry. You'd be no better than him then, and you are better. You're a good person, the best I know. Don't let hate make you no better than him."

It was right there at that moment that I fell in love with Annie Fleming. It hit me so hard I almost started to cry. I wanted to take her into my arms and hold her, protect her, erase her pain. I wanted to run away with her and start a life of our own. But I was thirteen and what did a thirteen-year-old know about making his way in the world? Instead, I said, "I hope we can be friends the rest of our lives."

Through her tears and red-rimmed eyes, she smiled at me. She had a beautiful smile. I always thought I could look at it all day and never get bored. "I'd like that, Ben." That was all she said, but it was enough to keep me going for five more years.

When I was eighteen I told Annie I loved her.

We'd remained friends through middle school and high school, the best of friends. She'd dated a few other guys and I'd gone out a couple times with other girls, but I think deep down we both knew we were destined for each other. Some day.

Our senior year I was accepted into the environmental science program at Penn State University. Annie never planned on going to college; she'd always said her only ambition was to be a wife and mommy. I couldn't have admired her more.

It was late August and we were standing in the driveway, me leaning against my jampacked F-150, when Annie walked over from her house. She didn't have a bruise on her. Her daddy had stopped beating on her when she became quick enough to dodge his blows and make him look foolish. Instead, he'd resorted to the verbal brand of abuse; I think he came over and took lessons from my father.

Annie's hair was swept back in a loose ponytail, and she wore a pair of jeans and a snug T-shirt, which accentuated her slender, athletic figure. Normally she smiled a lot when she was around me, but this time there was no smile.

"I can't believe you're actually leaving." She leaned against the door of the truck and folded her arms in a pouty kind of way.

I shoved my hands in my pockets. "I can't either. Kinda snuck up on me."

She patted the truck's rusty exterior. "You think this ole gal is up for the trip?"

I'd wondered too if my aging Ford would make the fifteen-hour trek north. "We'll find out, I guess. I may be calling you to come rescue me along the side of the highway somewhere in northern Virginia."

There was her smile. "I'd be there in a heartbeat."

"Even at two in the morning?"

"Even if you were halfway across the world."

A moment of comfortless silence hung between us while I suppose we both tried to put off the inevitable goodbye.

My palms had taken to sweating, and my pulse suddenly thumped in my ears. I hadn't planned on saying it, I was anything but impulsive, but it just seemed the time was right. I blurted the words out. "I love you, Annie."

If she was surprised by my awkward declaration she never showed it. She glanced at me then looked straight ahead. "I wondered when you'd get around to saying it."

"What?"

"Oh, c'mon, Ben. You've loved me since middle school. You know it."

"How could you tell?"

"A girl knows when she's loved."

"Really?"

She faked a look of surprise. "Guys can't tell?"

I shook my head. "We're clueless."

Annie slid closer to me, so close her arm touched mine. "Well, since you're so clueless I guess I have to spell it out for you. The feeling is mutual."

I was paralyzed. My mouth suddenly went dry. "Hmm." It was all I could muster.

She nudged me. "Is that all you're gonna say?"

Finally, my voice came. "How long?"

"How long what?"

"Have you felt this way?"

Another nudge, this time harder. She smiled again. "Ben Flurry, you act like it's some disease. I've loved you since we were thirteen, that time you threatened to kill my dad. I was so mad at you for saying it but at the same time I knew you only wanted to protect me. And I knew you'd always be the only one who'd ever want to protect me. It was probably the sweetest thing anyone's ever said to me. Until now."

I never told her that was the exact time I fell in love with her too. I figured I'd have all the time in the world to tell her.

Again, on impulse, I turned to face Annie, put my hands on her shoulders, and kissed her soundly on the lips. She didn't pull back, didn't push me away. Instead, she leaned in and returned my kiss.

We were married four years later, a month after I graduated and landed a job with the Pennsylvania Department of Environmental Protection. It was a simple wedding, outside with a picnic reception. Annie's parents offered to pay for a big fancy deal, spend thousands on their little girl, but Annie refused. She didn't want any part of her father's generosity, knowing it always came with a price. We lived in a two-bedroom apartment where the furniture was sparse but the smiles and laughs were abundant. We were happy and madly in love.

Two months after the wedding, I came home from work one rainy day and found Annie sitting on the floor of the bathroom crying. I feared the worst though I had no idea what the worst could be.

"Annie, what's wrong? What is it?"

She held up a little white stick and pointed to the pink lines. It was then I realized her tears were not tears of sorrow or pain but of happiness and expectancy.

The time rolled by and the months were filled with shopping for baby supplies and measuring Annie's growing belly. And as her belly grew so did her appetite. Late night runs to the local fast food joint became the norm. She'd sit up until midnight eating a greasy burger with French fries and watching the late-night shows.

One morning, three weeks before her due date, I was awakened by Annie jumping up and stumbling out of bed. "My water ... my water ..."

I stirred and turned over. At first I thought indigestion had finally gotten the best of her. But after feeling the wet sheets on her side of the bed I realized what had happened.

It was as if someone reached inside my head and flipped the panic switch. I was out of bed faster than my feet could find the floor and landed on my butt. The clock on the dresser said it was 4:52. The outside world was dark but rain tapped on the windows. It had been raining for four days straight and nearly every secondary road in our area was flooded. Alternate routes to the hospital ran through my mind. I hadn't planned for this, for our baby to be three weeks early. I wasn't prepared.

Fortunately, Annie was. She was calm too. She stood at the foot of the bed holding her belly, legs spread and glistening in the light of the small lamp. Sweat dappled her forehead and upper lip. "Ben, get the bag."

I found my legs, got them under me, and stood. "What bag?"

"The hospital bag. It has all my things in it and the baby's too." I didn't even know she'd gotten a bag together. "It's in the closet."

Bag in hand, I led my wife into the bathroom. "Call the doctor's office," she said as if she were giving directions to a five-year-old, "and tell them my water broke and we're on our way to the hospital. The number's on the fridge."

I left her standing in the bathroom and stumbled down the stairs to find the number.

The next few hours are still a blur. Somehow we got to the hospital. It took us all of six tries with different routes before we found one that wasn't flooded. Annie was given a room and things started happening. Contractions hit her hard and heavy. The nurses kept commenting on how well she was handling it for her first labor and how quickly things were progressing. We watched the monitor beside her bed, and I tried to prepare her for every contraction but she could feel them before I spotted the little line beginning to slope upward. The line below it was the baby's heart rate. It pulsed fast and steady ... until one particularly strong contraction hit Annie out of nowhere and the heartbeat slowed noticeably.

I pushed the button for a nurse and within minutes the room was full of people in scrubs hurrying about and talking in hushed tones. The doctor arrived soon after, all business and straight-faced. He had Annie lie back and checked her.

"Dear," he said, "you're fully dilated and effaced." And after glancing at the monitor and the sluggish pulse line, he looked at Annie and raised his eyebrows. "Okay, now, on the next contraction push with everything you have. We need to get this little darling out."

Annie pushed and strained until I thought the veins in her forehead and neck would pop. But not much happened. When the contraction passed she dropped her head back and panted like a woman who'd just run a marathon. Sweat stuck her hair to her forehead and ran rivulets down her cheeks.

Thank God a nurse was by her side to comfort and instruct her because I proved to be useless. I'm not usually squeamish about pain and body fluids and such, but there's something about watching your wife suffer that tears at your heart. I'm a fixer, a problem-solver, and this was one valley I couldn't carry her through. I gripped her hand and wiped her tears and prayed. Man, did I pray.

On the next contraction the doctor said he could see the top of the head.

Two contractions later, Annie let out a guttural moan and bore down.

I could have sworn the hands on the clock stood still at that moment and the world stopped spinning on its axis. I heard the doctor say something about notifying the NICU, heard one of the nurses let out a pitiful moan, heard Annie grunt and sigh deeply. But it was what I didn't hear that scared me. There was no crying. No sound of a healthy baby gasping for its first breaths of air. No sound of *life*. The doctor cut the umbilical and that's when I caught a glimpse of our baby girl, as blue as a Smurf, with the umbilical wrapped around her little neck like a tentacle from some otherworldly creature. She was as limp as a wet blanket in the doctor's big hands.

Annie kept saying, "What's wrong? Why isn't she crying?"

A nurse took our daughter, wrapped her in a blanket, and swept her away. At that moment I thought I felt the floor shift and almost lost my balance. My heart was in my mouth. I couldn't even speak. All I could do was take Annie in my arms and cry with her.

A little over a week later, I stood behind the glass doors at the rear of our house, the ones that overlooked the patio and a sprawling field, and held my daughter, Elizabeth Grace. Lizzy. She was beautiful, pink, plump, and fully alive. Our miracle. The doctors all told us she might have some cognitive deficiencies and motor control problems as she matured and developed because of the lack of oxygen to her brain during those harrowing minutes, but, at the time, we didn't care. She was our daughter and she was alive.

I loved the view out the back of our house. Where the green grass of the yard ended a corn field, harvested and ready for winter, spread out like a brown ocean for as far as I could see. I knew that beyond the horizon was a wood that ran the whole way to the neighboring farm because I'd walked it many a time. It was my place to be alone and think and pray, to allow the world to fade away and just be who I wanted to be, who I was born to be. Just Ben. No pressure, no expectations, no schedules or bosses or reports to finish.

I felt that way holding Lizzy too. To her, I was just Daddy, even though she didn't know it yet. I could look into those baby blues all day and see in them the kind of innocence and trust and faith the world of adults knew nothing of.

Annie came up behind me and kissed the back of my neck. "Hey, Daddy. Watcha doing?"

"Just admiring our perfect little baby girl."

She touched Lizzy's cheek with her finger. "She is perfect, isn't she?"

"I'm going to spoil her. You know that, don't you."

"I suspected as much."

"I've a right to."

"Every daddy does."

Annie rested her cheek on my arm and worked Lizzy's tiny hand around her finger.

My eyes lifted and found the horizon again. From our home to the edge of the world the sky was blue, streaked with wispy clouds and criss-crossing contrails. But beyond the horizon, a long, low, gray storm front inched closer like an army marching to battle. And at that moment I had the feeling that what we'd just been through was only the beginning. That some devious, malevolent force was tracking our happy little family, stalking us, gaining ever so slowly, intent on causing mayhem and leaving hearts broken.

I tightened my hold on Lizzy and tensed as if the force would suddenly materialize and snatch her from my arms.

Annie noticed and lifted her head. "What's wrong?"

"Nothing. Just my imagination toying with me." Only it wasn't.

CHAPTER 2

THE WEEKS AND MONTHS passed like the closing and opening of so many doors. Annie and I loved nothing more than watching Lizzy develop and grow and explore the world around her. I'd hold her in my arms and look into her eyes as she studied my face, every inch of it. Eventually, her hands took over the exploring duties and she'd squeeze my ears, my nose, and poke at my eyes. She seemed especially intrigued by the stubble on my chin and loved to scratch at it. Then she began investigating with her mouth and I'd wind up covered in baby drool in a matter of seconds.

Her first steps were in our kitchen. I'd arrived home from work late one evening and Annie was in the kitchen with Lizzy finishing dinner. Lizzy stood next to the counter, holding on to the leg of a barstool. When she saw me, she squealed and hollered "Daa!" and let go. Before she knew what she had done she'd taken three steps, stopped, squealed again, and waved her arms like she was trying to lift off and fly the rest of the way to me. The motion tipped her off balance and she promptly landed on her bottom and laughed and clapped her hands.

Setting my briefcase down, I lifted her into my arms and kissed her on the forehead.

Annie clapped. "Her first steps," she said, wiping at the tears that had gathered in her eyes. "You know, I hadn't even thought about what the doctors in the hospital said until now."

"What's that?"

"About her having motor control problems."

I hadn't thought about it either. Lizzy had developed normally, lifting her head when she should, rolling over, sitting up. The pediatrician never mentioned a word about her being developmentally slow or challenged or whatever the politically correct term was. To us she was Lizzy, our healthy, strong baby girl.

"Nah," I said. "She's as strong as a horse. A baby one." I held Lizzy close and kissed her chunky cheek.

Lizzy blew raspberries, dragged her hand across her mouth, then wiped her drool on my cheek.

I set Lizzy on her feet and watched her balance, take a few steps, teeter, and fall on her padded bottom again. She twisted up her face, looked at me, and started to cry.

"I have that effect on a lot of women." I lifted Lizzy into my arms again.

"What's that?" Annie winked. "They cry when they look at you?"

"No, the falling over part."

"Yeah, right."

"Well you fell for me, didn't you?"

Annie shook the wooden spoon in her hand at me and smiled. "It wasn't as long of a fall as you'd like to think."

"Good one."

Lizzy stopped crying and held my face in her hands and squeezed my cheeks. "Da."

I kissed her again on her forehead then her cheek. "Yes, baby girl, I'm home now."

She wrapped her arms around my neck and squeezed.

***

One of the only things I remember my father doing with me as a child was holding me on his lap while he drove the lawn tractor around our little plot of land in North Carolina. Neither the yard nor the tractor were much to speak of and the yard could have easily been mowed with a push mower, but dad liked the feel of sitting atop that old John Deere and it humming and sputtering under his butt. I liked it too. It was better than any twenty-five-cent carnival ride because with the vibration of the engine came that distant feeling of danger. There were some sharp blades rotating below us and ours wouldn't have been the first toes or fingers severed in those whirling knives. More than spending time with my dad (and the fact that he was usually sober when he mowed), I liked the adventure of riding the mower, blazing a trail through the overgrown grass. I'd imagine we were explorers plowing through some faraway jungle underbrush, discovering new land and soon to run into its very inhospitable inhabitants.

So when Lizzy was five, I decided she was old enough to do a ride along. Annie protested—she wouldn't have been a good mother if she hadn't—but I assured her that I knew what I was doing, that I was completely sober (I'd, in fact, never been drunk a day in my life, never even tasted a cold beer), and that I had Lizzy's safety first and foremost on my mind. Reluctantly, she agreed and watched from the window the entire time, her arms crossed and chin raised.

At first, Lizzy wasn't too sure about the mower. She looked it over like it was some long-extinct dinosaur that was not to be trusted. "Daddy," she finally said, "are you sure this is okay?" She looked back at the kitchen window where her mother stood like a prison guard keeping watch over the inmates.

"Sure it is, sweetheart." I took her into my arms and lifted her onto my lap. "I'd never let anything happen to you."

With one arm around her waist, I started the mower. Lizzy jumped and pressed her tense body against mine. Once the mower got going, though, she relaxed and rested one hand on my arm.

I thought again of those rotating blades. As an adult I knew they were perfectly safe as long as we stayed on the upside of the mower. But the thought of them spinning like they do ... I tightened my hold on Lizzy and kissed the top of her head. I was her daddy, her protector, her knight, and swore right then and there that I'd do everything in my power to make sure she never suffered. But life is life and suffering is part of it. And that suffering would certainly one day find my daughter.

I just never thought it would be so soon.

***

The next year, Lizzy started first grade. After much discussion and prayer both Annie and I decided it would be best to homeschool her. Annie felt up to the challenge and I certainly didn't question her ability. She was one of the most intelligent, level-headed people I knew. I often kidded her that I married her for her brain. Everyone should keep a smarty around, especially when *Jeopardy* was on.

All summer Annie prepared, researched different curricula, and talked to others who had taken the homeschool route. And all summer, Lizzy's excitement built. So when the big day came it was quite the ordeal indeed. Annie and Lizzy both got up early and Annie made a first-day-of-school breakfast of pancakes and eggs and sausage.

Before I left for work I kissed Lizzy on the cheek then Annie on the lips. "You ready for this?"

"As ready as I'm ever gonna be."

"Her education is in your hands you know. Her whole future. If she doesn't nail first grade she'll go through the rest of her life not being able to add two and two."

Annie punched me in the arm. "Nothing like a little pressure on the first day. Thanks a lot."

I kissed her again. "You'll do great and so will she. You two are perfect together." And they were. They were like two parts to the same gear, in perfect sync, always complementing each other. Lizzy was a miniature version of Annie. Same smile, same laugh, same hands, right down to the way they both puckered their lips when they were in deep concentration.

"Let's just hope we haven't knocked each other out by the time you get home."

"Fat chance of that happening."

She smiled. "But there is a chance."

I left and called home almost every hour during the day, not to make sure they were both conscious but because I missed being there, missed this milestone in both of their lives.

When I got home I already knew they'd had a great day. Lizzy ran at me holding a piece of paper in her hands. "Look, Daddy, I can read big words."

I kissed Annie and took the paper in my hand. It had four words in bold print next to a corresponding picture.

Lizzy pulled my arm down. "Watch this." The pride beamed from her eyes. She pointed to the first word. "Animal."

"Wow. That's exactly right."

Her finger directed my attention to the following words. "Arrow. Above. Across."

I shook my head. "I can't believe it. One day of school and you can already read like this? You must have a really good teacher."

Lizzy folded her hands at her chest. "Mommy's the best teacher in the whole wide world." Then she turned and took off running out of the kitchen.

Annie slung a dish towel over her shoulder, leaned against the counter and smiled at me.

"I'm glad your first day went so well," I said.

She turned both palms up. "We're both still alive."

"Oh, c'mon, it was better than that." I crossed the kitchen and took her into my arms. She smelled like garlic and onions. Spaghetti sauce was simmering on the stove.

"All right. It was great. We had so much fun together. I think we're doing the right thing."

"I know we are." I kissed her and pulled her close, wishing life would never advance from this moment.

After dinner I patted my stomach and leaned back in my chair. "Delicious, honey. Best spaghetti I ever had."

Annie gave me a sideways glance. "It's the same recipe I always use."

"But today is special and that makes everything taste better. In fact, I can only think of one thing that would top this day off and make it truly perfect."

Lizzy's eyes widened. "What's that, Daddy?"

I leaned forward and touched her nose. "Ice cream."

Annie frowned. "We don't have any in the freezer."

"I know. Let's go out."

Lizzy jumped out of her chair. "Can we go to Buster's?" Buster's was a local ice cream parlor boasting some of the best homemade ice cream in Pennsylvania.

"Buster's it is. And I know what flavor you're going to get."

"No you don't," Lizzy said.

"Yup, the same kind you always get, cotton candy."

"Wrong."

Annie stood and started to clear the table. "Oh, I bet you'll change your mind when you get there and go with the cotton candy."

"Well," Lizzy tapped her finger to her mouth. "It is my favorite."

"Of course," I said. "I knew it all along."

Outside, a steady rain had begun falling and the heavy cloud cover brought an early sunset. The sky was charcoal gray and the world a shimmery landscape of muted shapes and dark shadows. As I drove I thought of how fast the past seven years had hurried by. I thought of the days spent in the hospital following Lizzy's birth, the prayers said, the tears cried. There were times when I questioned if my little girl would ever see the first day of first grade.

Annie was turned around in the front seat talking to Lizzy but I wasn't paying close enough attention to make out what she was saying. My mind was on other things, sentimental things. Soon Lizzy would be starting middle then high school. Boys would come next, knocking on our door, and I would no longer be the number one man in my daughter's life. She'd want her independence, go to college, get married, and all I'd have is a brain full of memories and an empty room in my heart.

From outside the car came the noxious sound of a horn blowing, tires screeching, sliding, jolting me from my thoughts.

Annie screamed.

I didn't even see the semi's headlights.

CHAPTER 3

....

WHEN I WAS NINE I fell from my treehouse and broke my wrist. My mom took me to Boomer General Hospital and we sat there in that waiting room for nearly three hours, my wrist thumping, pain zinging up my arm all the way to the shoulder. I remember it well, everything about it. The sounds of the sirens outside and the receptionist calling people's names. The guy in the corner, doubled over with both arms crossed in front of his belly. He moaned so loudly I thought he was about to have a baby. His head was big and bald and pocked like a chunk of Swiss cheese. After one particularly enthusiastic moan he jumped up and ran to the bathroom, but the door was locked so he went ahead and barfed right there on the floor next to the water fountain. I remember the smells of that waiting room too, the sweat and antiseptic mingled with the pungent odor of Cheesehead's vomit.

When they finally did call my name, my mother jumped up and gave the receptionist an earful of down-home cussing. It wasn't her fault, we all knew that, but Mom needed someone to vent her anger and frustration on and that poor receptionist was the first warm body she encountered. I imagine she went home that evening and slid into a bathtub full of warm water, closed her eyes, and tried to forget about her job and the crazy lady who taught her a new vocabulary.

***

I awoke in a hospital room at night. The windows were dark and there was only one small light that dusted the room in a muted glow. That smell was there too, sweat and antiseptic. My head was a ball of fog and I had no idea why I was there. The clock on the wall said it was 2:35. It's quite disorienting to awaken in a strange place in the middle of the night. I tried to sit up but a searing pain in my head pushed me back down. I lifted my hand and found a thick bandage wrapped around the entire circumference of my head. Pressing on it, I found no particularly tender spots. I tried to think back, to recreate the events of my life right before I blacked out. At least I assumed I'd blacked out, but I had no memory. It was as if the slate of my brain had been wiped clean. I did remember going to work, that it was Lizzy's first day of school. I remembered what I did at work, the farms I'd visited, the way Mrs. Branson had offered me tea like she always does. I remembered how good her tea was too, like it always was. I came home, we had dinner, spaghetti, then we went out for ice cream. But that's where it stopped. I couldn't remember if we'd actually had ice cream or not. What flavor did I get? How about Lizzy and Annie?

I closed my eyes and concentrated. What happened after we left the house? From the fact that I was in a hospital room with my head bandaged like a mummy's I deduced that there must have been some kind of accident. Suddenly, panic gripped my chest with bony hands and squeezed. Where were Annie and Lizzy?

Rooting around the bed with my hand, ignoring the pain in my head, I found the call button for the nurse and pressed it. A few seconds later a young nurse opened the door and entered the room. "Hello there, Mr. Flurry; I'm Rose. I'll be your nurse for the rest of the night. How are you feeling?"

There was something in her eyes, something in the tone of her voice that I didn't like. Was it pity? Sadness? I couldn't tell.

"Where's my wife and daughter?" I reached for the bandage and touched it. "What happened?"

Rose looked back at me like I'd asked her what the capital of South Dakota was. "Uh, I'll get the doctor. He told me to let him know when you woke up."

She spun to leave but I stopped her. "Wait, Rose, please ... what happened? Were we in an accident?"

Rose turned slowly and faced me. Yes, it was sadness in her eyes.

Deep, profound sadness. And for an instant I didn't want her to answer my question. They say ignorance is bliss and at a moment like that I couldn't agree more. Rose nodded. "Yes, you were in an accident."

"Where's my wife and daughter? Annie and Elizabeth Flurry. Are they okay?"

She hesitated, enough that I knew the answer before she said anything. I almost stopped her, told her she didn't need to say it, I didn't really want to know, but I didn't because I knew I needed to know. Ignorance may be bliss but the bliss only lasts for a short time, then it's a curse. "I should really get the doctor."

"No! I'm sorry." I pulled my head up and pleaded with her. "Please, Rose, you can tell me."

What I didn't know and learned much later was that that was Rose Grimey's first day on the job. She was fresh out of school, graduated only a few weeks prior. Some welcome into the nursing world.

She paused again and bit her lower lip. She had a nice face, soft around the edges, big eyes, high brow. She walked to the bed and placed a hand on my head. Her touch was soft and caring. "Lay back, Mr. Flurry—"

"It's Ben. Call me Ben."

She forced a smile and that's when I saw the tears in her eyes. "Ben, you need your rest."

I did as she ordered. "Where's my wife and daughter?"

Rose sucked in a deep breath and blew it out. "You're in Hershey. You were medevaced here after an auto accident."

"All three of us?"

She nodded. "Your daughter is in the ICU."

"And Annie, where is she? Is she okay?"

A tear pushed its way out from the corner of Rose's eye and caught on the flare of her nostril. Her chin quivered. She shook her head and whispered, "I'm sorry."

"Sorry for what?" I didn't want her to answer. *Please don't answer.*

"She ... she didn't make it."

***

27

Bruce Gibbons was the biggest kid in the fifth grade. He was eleven and had a mustache and weighed nearly a hundred and fifty pounds. And for some reason Bruce hated me. I had no idea why; I'd never done anything to warrant his contempt. But in fifth grade kids didn't need a reason for doing anything and Bruce certainly fit that bill. One day, a few weeks after school had started, Bruce approached me on the playground. I was minding my own business like I usually did, throwing dirt clods at the big oak that sat at the far end of the lot. He had his shoulders back and chest out. With one hand he smoothed his mustache and with the other he picked up a clod.

"Hey, Benny. What, you think you're Nolan Ryan or something?"

I held a clod in my hand but didn't say anything. I knew that to answer Bruce was to challenge him. There was no correct response.

"You think you can throw better than me, wimp?"

Again, I didn't answer.

Bruce stepped up and pointed to a low hanging limb. "See that limb there? Bet you can't hit it and I can."

When I didn't accept his challenge, he nudged me with his elbow. "Go on, give it a toss. Let's see what you're made of. Wimp."

Not wanting to fight Bruce with hands, I figured if I could beat him in dirt clod throwing I might earn at least a little respect. Surely, even in the code of bully conduct, there's room for giving credit where it's due. I shrugged, aimed, cocked my arm, and let that clod fly. It traveled a perfect arc and hit the limb square, exploding into a cloud of dust. I was impressed by my own ability.

Bruce sniffed. "Wimp's luck. Watch this."

He swung his arm back like a catapult and released the dirt clod at the perfect time. It sailed through the air and missed the limb by a whole foot, landing on the ground a good twenty feet beyond the tree.

He stared at that limb for a full ten seconds, clenching his jaw, before turning to face me. I think he was just as surprised as I was that he'd missed. I thought for sure he'd offer me some compliment or a clap on the back, but instead he reared back, balled his hand into a fist, and buried it in my stomach. I doubled over, dropped to my knees, and rolled to my side. Nausea radiated out from my abdomen and forced bile into my mouth. A knot the size of a basketball formed in my gut.

Bruce stood over me like the last standing gladiator. "You're not better than me, wimp. Just remember that." Then he walked away and left me there to suffer alone.

I learned two things that day. One, getting hit in the stomach is no fun. And two, never let your guard down.

***

As I lay in that hospital bed, totally helpless and unable to do anything, I had that basketball-sized knot in my stomach again, just like when Bruce Gibbons landed his meaty hand in my abdomen. And the taste of bile was in my mouth.

I closed my eyes to shut off the tears, but they came anyway.

Rose took my hand in hers. She hadn't been a nurse long enough to be calloused to other folks' trials yet. "I'm so sorry, Mr. ... Ben. I'm going to get the doctor now."

I opened my eyes. "Wait, what about Lizzy? How is she?"

Another tear slipped from Rose's eye, then another. "She has two broken legs, pretty bad. She's comfortable now and scheduled for surgery in the morning. I'm sorry."

"You can stop apologizing," I said. "You didn't do this."

Things were coming back to me slowly, in pieces, like an old film strip that'd been spliced together. But the timing was all off. I remembered driving in the rain; I hated driving in the rain. The way the water absorbs the light and makes everything darker. The way the headlights of oncoming traffic glare on the windshield. I remembered leaving the house and asking Lizzy what kind of ice cream she wanted. Cotton candy. It was always cotton candy. I remembered Annie turning around in her seat to say something to Lizzy. She was beautiful, the prettiest woman I'd ever met. I was the luckiest man alive. I loved her like crazy. I remembered her scream, the sound of tires skidding, the blast of a horn. And that was it.

I pulled my hand away from Rose. "Can you leave me alone now?"

"Sure." She stepped back. "Your pastor was here earlier to visit you and Lizzy."

Annie and I had recently left the church we'd been attending for nearly four years. They'd gone through some changes we just couldn't agree with and, after voicing our opinion, we were asked to leave. That was a month ago. We'd visited a couple churches but hadn't found anything yet to call home. Friends we'd had there were suddenly no longer friendly. Apparently the church leadership had pinned the differences we shared squarely on our shoulders and painted us as troublemakers. It hurt plenty at the time and the wounds were still healing, but we were getting over it, learning to deal with the disappointment so easily found in others if you looked for it. We were learning to forgive. That Pastor Rich had come to visit was a little surprising. Perhaps he'd needed to work through some guilt or regret for the way we were so easily dismissed. Regardless, it did give me a little comfort knowing he'd stopped by. I nodded at Rose. "Okay. Thanks."

She paused as if she wanted to say something else, something encouraging or helpful or maybe just to apologize again. Instead she said, "I'll let the doctor know you're awake."

"Sure." I turned my head toward the window. Numbness overtook my body and I was suddenly very tired. I'd just found out my wife was dead and my daughter was in the ICU with two broken legs and all I wanted to do was sleep. That was when I let the tears come. I just opened up the dam and let the water flow. Sobs racked my body. I'm sure if anyone was in the hallway they heard me, but I didn't care. An image of holding Lizzy tight while watching a storm front move in flashed through my mind. I'd promised then and again on that mower to protect her always, to never let anything bad happen to her. That front had finally caught up to us and I'd broken my promise.

As I lay there staring at the darkened window, my eyelids grew heavy. So heavy I couldn't hold them open any longer and finally succumbed to sleep.

CHAPTER 4

DESPITE MY FATHER'S PROPENSITY for alcohol, he dragged us to church every Sunday. It was the one day he went nearly a whole day without a drink. *Nearly* the whole day. When I was tucked into bed I'd lie there and hear the TV flip on and that familiar *psst* of the pop top being peeled off. Dad always wore a tie to church and insisted I did too. He said it was only proper to dress in a dignified manner when going to the house of the Lord.

We attended the Boomer First Baptist Church, where everyone else in our little town went. There was only one other church in town, St. Olivia's Catholic Church, and it didn't stand a chance in the South against a white, clapboard-sided Baptist church with a steeple and bell. Every Sunday morning the double doors of the BFBC stood wide open and the citizens of Boomer poured in. An hour and a half later they poured out, most of them unchanged but at least satisfied that they'd done their weekly duty.

Every year we had a week-long revival come to town. It was always the same guy, Pastor Gilbert Flowers, and he'd set up his big white tent down by the river and for five nights would holler and sweat and pace back and forth. His message was all hellfire and brimstone with an equal serving of both. Pastor Flowers was a big man, round in the middle with a face as large as a dinner platter and all pushed in like a bulldog's. He grew his hair long on one side and combed it over to hide the bald spot on top. But when he got going and started his singsong ranting and pacing and sweating, that hair would flip and flop like a lame wing on a bird. I liked him, though, because he was interesting to watch and listen to. A nice change from the monotonous drone I heard every Sunday morning from Pastor Withers.

On the last day of the revival meetings, Pastor Flowers would march everyone down to the Cape Fear River and spend a good part of the evening dunking them into the cold waters one by one. I swam in those waters and dunked myself plenty of times. I often wondered what was so special about the way Pastor Flowers did it.

The summer of my eighth year, the revival came to town like it always did and I attended every meeting like I always did. My mother insisted we all go, even my dad.

Pastor Flowers spent the first four nights hollering at us about repentance and confession and salvation. He said God loved us and didn't want us to spend eternity separated from Him but that if we died without repenting, without confessing our sins and seeking His forgiveness, that that was exactly what was going to happen. Dying without salvation didn't sound like too good of an idea to me. According to Pastor Flowers it meant there would only be one thing waiting for me on the other side. Fire and torment. I didn't like the sound of that.

At the end of the meeting on the fourth night, when the altar call was given and Miss Parrot played "Shall We Gather at the River?" I went forward. I didn't want to and actually fought it, but it was as if I had no control over my legs and they just moved on their own. Whether I wanted to go forward or not was irrelevant at that moment. I knew I *needed* to. One step at a time I walked that aisle on numb legs, past many of the folks I'd known my whole life. It was a hot night and the sweat poured down my back and chest.

At the front of the tent, I stood with about ten other folk, some I knew, some I didn't, and Pastor Flowers spoke to each one of us. When he got to me he leaned forward and put his big, fat hand on my shoulder. His face glistened with sweat that ran down off his forehead, over his face, down his neck, and soaked his shirt collar.

"Son," he said. "Do you know what you're doing up here?" His double chin jiggled when he talked. I hadn't noticed that from the back of the tent.

I nodded.

"Tell me, son. Tell me why you came forward."

"For—for salvation."

He clapped my shoulder. "Yes, that's right. For the Lord's salvation. Do you repent of your sins? Do you confess before the Lord?"

I nodded again. And I did. I was only eight but I knew exactly what I was doing. I'd sinned and offended God. That wasn't good and would only end in a very bad way if I didn't make it right.

Pastor Flowers leaned in closer and I saw the yellow of his eyes. "Do you receive Christ as your savior? Do you make him Lord of your heart and life?"

I swallowed hard. "Yes."

He studied me for a moment. His little beady eyes scanned my face as if he could look past the exterior and see the real me, see if I was telling the truth or not. Then he said, "I believe you do. Yes, sir, I believe you do." He winked. "Amen, little brother. Amen!" He stood to his full height, which was a little taller than my dad, and proclaimed loudly. "Amen, brothers and sisters, another sheep has entered the fold."

A chorus of amens arose from the crowd of a couple hundred. Then Pastor Flowers led the entire assembly out of the tent and down to the river's bank. The Cape Fear River was not very wide nor deep at this location, and it moved slow and steady, taking its time to wind through the terrain of central North Carolina. Dad said it was slower and lazier than a three-legged cow. I'd never seen a three-legged cow but figured he knew what he was talking about. Dad may have been a drunk but he knew a lot about a lot of different things.

On the river's bank, Pastor Flowers waded out about fifteen feet until the water was up to his waist. It had rained pretty hard a few mornings prior and the water was still brown and deeper than usual. "People of the Lord," he said. His voice was high-pitched but loud and skipped over the water like a smooth stone. "Form a line on the bank there if you wish to come into the water and be cleansed."

I looked at that water, at the dirt particles floating in it, and wondered how anyone could be cleaned in it, but I suspected Pastor Flowers wasn't talking about a physical cleaning. We needed to have our sins washed away. It sounded like a good idea to me so I broke free from my mother's hand and took a few steps forward through the crowd, glancing around to see how many others would line up first. A few people made their way to the water's edge and waited.

"You there." Pastor Flowers' voice pierced the quietness. I looked up and found he was pointing at me. "Young man, yes. Do you want to be baptized? Do you want to be cleansed?"

I walked to the water's edge and hesitated. Something about entrusting myself to this man made me suddenly nervous. I swam in the river lots of times and was a good swimmer but for some reason I now found myself afraid of the water. Two hands touched my shoulders and a voice whispered into my ear, "It's okay, Benjamin, go on now." It was Mrs. Leedy, my Sunday school teacher.

Step by step I made my way to Pastor Flowers, that cold water inching up my legs, to my crotch, to my belly. Finally, I stood next to him with the slow-moving water around my chest. He put his arm around my shoulders and smiled. "Son, did you mean what you did back there in the tent?"

"Yes, I did."

"Then," he moved around to my side and took my hands in his, keeping the other hand on my back, "I baptize you in the name of the Father, the Son, and the Holy Spirit."

Before I knew it I was under water, plunged deep into that dark river, the coldness surrounding me, flowing around me and through my hair and clothes. It lasted only a second before I broke the surface again and felt the warm sun on my skin. Pastor Flowers laughed as I wiped the water from my eyes and face and smoothed back my hair. The assembly on the river's bank broke into applause and offered up a cheer of amens. I found my mother in the crowd; she was smiling from cheek to cheek.

After the baptism, I went home and took a bath.

***

I awoke sometime in the morning to find a large black man standing at the foot of my bed. He was bald, big, and wore a white T-shirt and blue jeans. Muscles bulged beneath his shirt and the faint outline of an intricate tattoo covered the upper portion of his right arm. An ebony Mr. Clean.

"Mornin', son," he said and nodded at me. He looked old enough to be my father but there was no way I could have been his son.

I tried to push myself up but pain shot through my head, causing me to wince.

"Here." The big guy came around to the side of the bed and pushed the button to raise the head end. "Say when."

At about a forty-five-degree angle, I raised a hand. The bed stopped. "What are you doing here?" I didn't want to sound rude but am sure it came out that way.

"Just prayin' for ya. Hope that's all right. Any man who's goin' through what you're goin' through could use some prayer."

"Who are you?"

He clasped his hands behind his back. "Name's Tom."

I reached for my head, felt the bandage and the tenderness beneath it. "My head—"

"Pain medication's wearin' off. I'll go tell the nurse." He turned and left the room before I could stop him.

A few seconds later Rose walked in. "I hear your head is bothering you."

"How's Lizzy?"

"She's in surgery right now. Here." She gave me a little plastic cup with two pills in it. "For the pain. It's potent stuff."

I took the pills and downed them with a swig of water. "I want to see her as soon as she wakes up."

"Absolutely. How are you doing this morning?"

I looked at her and saw the innocence in her eyes. It was obvious she'd never lost anyone close to her. "My wife is gone." It was blunt, yes, but she needed to hear it. A memory of Annie holding Lizzy when she was just an infant ran through my mind and put tears in my eyes.

Rose backed away. "I'm sorry. I didn't mean to—"

"No, it's okay. When can I leave?" I had things to do, family to notify, a funeral to plan. They were the last things on my mind but nevertheless needed to be thought of. I was an only child and rarely talked to my parents and Annie only had one sister, two years older, who ran off to California with some rocker and no one had heard from in years. Annie never talked to her parents.

"The doctor stopped by while you were sleeping. He should be around soon."

"What time did they take Lizzy in?"

Rose glanced at her watch. "Six thirty. They said it would be a four- to five-hour surgery."

"It's that bad?"

She hesitated.

"Rose, tell me."

"Her legs were crushed. Multiple fractures in both of them. I'm sorry." She took another step backward, toward the door. "Listen, I'm going off my shift in ten minutes. Maya will be your nurse for most of the day. She's really nice."

"Thanks, Rose. For everything." She was exactly the nurse I needed.

"You're welcome. Okay then, bye."

She turned for the door but I stopped her. "Rose."

"Yes?"

"Don't ever stop caring, okay?"

She smiled. "I won't."

"But you might. As the years go by, the calluses will form and you won't care anymore. It'll just be a job. Don't let that happen."

"I won't."

Something told me she was telling the truth. She turned again.

"Rose."

"Yes?"

"Who was the big guy in here? Tom."

"Tom James. He's one of the maintenance guys."

"How did he know about me?"

She shrugged. "I don't know."

"Okay. Thanks."

Rose left and I was once again alone with my thoughts, my memories, my pain.

CHAPTER 5

THEY TOLD ME I had a severe concussion, grade three, that when they brought me in I was unconscious and vomiting. Pretty serious stuff. Fortunately, to their surprise, that's all that was wrong with me. No broken bones, no internal bleeding. Just some bruises and scrapes, mostly on my arms and legs. My wife and daughter took the brunt of the impact.

The doctor who visited was a young guy, short and stocky with thick glasses and a balding head. He had some kind of accent but I couldn't place it. Something European. Maybe Russian. He paced around the room and barely made eye contact. I didn't like him. He said they were going to keep me a few more days for observation then release me if all went well. I didn't care if they kept me a few more months, I just wanted to see my daughter, my Lizzy, then take her and disappear for a while. I didn't want to deal with the outside world, the mourners, the well-wishers, the cards and visits. Annie and I had no friends to speak of; we'd lost them all in the church debacle. They'd all proven to be fair-weather friends, the kind who suddenly find you expendable when your view of the world—or church—isn't the same as theirs. But there were those we considered acquaintances who would want to pay their respects, offer condolences, maybe make meals, that sort of thing. They'd mean well but I didn't want any part of what they'd have to offer. Not at the moment, anyway.

After the doctor left I put my face in the pillow and cried. I cried so hard I gave myself the dry heaves. Part of me didn't want to go on living without Annie, didn't want to go back to our home and sleep in our bed and prepare food in our kitchen. I didn't want to use our bathroom and see all her toiletries. I didn't want to sit on our back porch and see the gardens she'd worked so hard on. Another part of me just wanted to hold Lizzy. She was all I had left and she was so much like Annie. Through my daughter, a part of my wife would always remain. I wanted to be with Lizzy, to see her, to comfort her, cry with her. To smell Annie on her and see Annie in her eyes, her smile, hear her in her voice and laughter.

The door of the room opened and a young Pilipino nurse entered. She was short and had a round, kind face with bright, expressive eyes. A big smile. "Good morning, Mr. Flurry. I'm Maya, I'll be your nurse until evening. Do you need anything?"

There was only one thing I needed. "Is my daughter out of surgery yet?"

"I'll check."

She left and I stared at the black TV screen. I thought of turning it on, passing the time with a movie or the news, but the thought of anything but Annie and Lizzy entering my mind was almost blasphemous.

A minute later Maya came back. "She's in recovery and should be back in her room in about thirty minutes."

"I want to see her."

"I've already called for an orderly to come get you with a wheelchair and take you to her."

I liked Maya.

***

Lizzy's ICU room was small and crowded with beeping and humming machines. The overhead lights were dim but the tiny red and green LED bulbs and digital numbers on the monitors looked like a Christmas tree set-up. But the feel in the room was anything but festive. Lizzy looked so small in that bed, so helpless, so broken. She was asleep when the orderly—he'd introduced himself as simply "T"—rolled me in and parked me beside her bed. More tears came then. I tried to hold them back, tried to be strong in case Lizzy woke up, but there was no stopping them. I took her hand in mine and ran my thumb over her fingers. A scab had already formed over a cut on her thumb. She also had a bruise along the right side of her face that stretched from eye to jawline.

But her legs were the worst. Her right leg was supported in a metal fixator with long screws penetrating the flesh at various locations and angles. Bruises and incisions discolored the swollen limb. Her left leg was heavily bandaged from hip to toes.

How was I to do this? How was I to care for my daughter? She needed a mother. I was not equipped to instruct her in the ways of womanhood. I could barely put her hair in a ponytail. What would happen when she got older, started changing, becoming a woman, got interested in boys? All these thoughts trudged through the fog in my head, tormented me. And suddenly I was overcome with anger, rage even. How could this happen to us? How could—

A light knock on the door startled me.

A man stood there, tall, thick in the midsection, full graying beard and deep-set, dark eyes. He wore a white lab coat that reached to his knees.

"Mr. Flurry?"

"Yes, Ben."

He approached and stuck out his hand. "I'm Dr. Ostervan. I did the work on your daughter's legs."

"Oh." I glanced again at Lizzy's badly damaged legs. "Thank you. How bad were they?"

He raised both eyebrows and dropped them. "Pretty bad. I wasn't sure we were going to be able to save the right one. It was nearly severed just below the knee. But someone's prayers were heard because it all came together nicely. The left one wasn't as bad but things were still touch and go. She lost a lot of blood too. When she came in we couldn't operate right away because of the swelling and blood loss."

"Thank you for what you did. What happens from here?"

Dr. Ostervan sighed. "Well, immediately, we keep her here for a few more days, then move her to the orthopedic floor for a few days, then she goes to the rehab hospital until we can take the fixator off. Then it's home. More rehab. Possibly more surgeries."

"More surgeries?" I hated the idea of my baby going through this again.

"Depends on how the legs grow and develop. The growth plates were compromised on both of the tibias and the right femur. We'll keep a close eye on things as she matures."

I took Lizzy's hand again. "Will she be able to walk?"

Dr. Ostervan placed his hand on my shoulder and squeezed. "I'm confident she'll walk again, maybe with a limp, but she'll walk."

"Thank you, Doctor."

When he left I kissed Lizzy's hand. How would I tell her about Annie, her mommy? Weren't her legs enough to deal with? She didn't need that kind of news too. She'd be devastated. How could I be strong for her when I was a ball of sobbing mush myself? As much as I loved Lizzy and hurt for her and wanted to protect her, I had to get away for a moment, I had to sort this through in my own mind. I wheeled myself out of the room and found the orderly in the small waiting room reading a magazine.

"Hey, can you tell me where the chapel is?"

"T" closed the magazine and jumped up. "You got it, Mistah Flurry." He grabbed the grips on the wheelchair.

"I can walk, you know. Just tell me where it is."

"Oh, no, Mistuh Flurry. I can't let you do that. This is my job. It's your job to sit back and enjoy the ride."

I don't know why I wanted to go to the chapel. Maybe because it's where people go to grieve, to think, to sort out their emotions. Maybe because it's the most quiet, peaceful place in the hospital, the only place where you can escape the sterile, whitewashed, antiseptic environment. Or maybe because it's where I'd feel closest to God, and it was with Him that I had a grievance.

Whatever the reason, I was there, in a pew, my arms resting on the pew in front of me. I was the only one in there and, though it was small, I felt as though I could get lost and forgotten about. And the anger was there again too. Why did this happen to us? Why us? *Why did you let this happen, God?*

Memories shot through my mind again: the wet and glassy road, the feel of the steering wheel under my hands, the darkness that loomed just beyond the muted light of the car's headlamps. Annie's voice, Lizzy's laughter. I turn to look at Annie ... she's beautiful and so full of life. A flash of lights, horn blaring, tires skidding like sandpaper being dragged along rough wood. I didn't remember the impact and violence that followed it and was glad for it. I didn't want to remember that. The memories I had would haunt me enough.

I wasn't sure I yet fully accepted the fact that Annie was gone. She wouldn't be waiting for us at home. There would be no more hugs, no more kisses, no more holding hands and laughing together. No more arguing, no more making up. It seemed like such a foreign concept. She'd been part of my life since kindergarten and now she was no more.

The tears came again, fast and furious, and wracked my frame with sobs. Turning my head toward the vaulted ceiling of the chapel I shut my eyes and shook my fist at God. "Why," I whispered. "*Why*? Why *her*? God, I want her back. Please don't do this to me. You raised Lazarus, give me back my wife."

I fell silent then and bowed my head as more tears pushed their way out of my eyes. I don't know how long I sat there but eventually I felt someone slide in the pew next to me. Opening my eyes, I found Tom there, elbows on his knees, head in his hands.

"What are you doing here?" I asked. My voice was hoarse from crying.

Tom looked up. "Prayin' for you, son."

"How'd you know I was here?"

"Isn't this where folks go to feel closer to God? Whether to pray to him or holler at him?"

I wiped the tears from my cheeks and looked straight ahead. "I think I'm doing more hollering than praying."

"Don't blame ya. I'd be hollerin' too."

"Do you think it's wrong?"

He turned his head toward me. "What's that?"

"Hollering at God."

"Depends why your hollerin' and what you're saying. God, he understands the cries of a broken heart. He's been there." He paused, dipped the corners of his mouth, and nodded his head slowly. "Yep, I think God is a big enough God that he can take a little rantin' and ravin' from us. He knows your heart, son, and he loves you more than you could ever love him back. He knows this is somethin' you're gonna need to wrestle with a bit." His big hand patted my leg. "You just keep on wrestlin', you hear? Can't promise you'll get your answer but it's in the wrestling that we learn to surrender."

"You sound like you speak from experience."

"Yes, sir." Tears pooled in Tom's eyes and he swallowed hard. "Yes, sir, I do. Lost my wife and son some nineteen years ago. House fire. I wasn't even home. I was at the church preparin' for my next sermon. I could have been home, though. I could have prepared at home but thought there were always too many interruptions." A tear spilled out of his eye and tracked a path down his dark cheek. It glistened like mercury in the chapel's lighting. "Yes, sir, I did my own wrestling after that. Even left my church behind because of it. What I would give now for even one of those interruptions."

"Did you get your answer?"

He shook his head. "Nope. Don't think I ever will. But that's okay 'cause I know God has a plan. If I was still at my church and still had my family I never would have met you."

I turned and found him smiling wide at me, tears streaming down his cheeks.

"Hardly a good trade-off," I said.

"I suppose it isn't." He patted my leg again. "Son, work it out then let it go. Bitterness won't do you or your daughter no good. She needs you. She lost her momma. She needs her daddy just like you need yours." He pointed to the ceiling.

But I was already bitter and angry, and not just angry but downright mad. Both at God and myself.

CHAPTER 6

························

Lizzy woke up at exactly 6:05 in the evening. I was sitting by her bed, dozing, when I heard her sweet little voice.

"Daddy?"

I rubbed the sleep from my face and smoothed back her hair with the palm of my hand. "Hey, baby girl. I'm here. How do you feel?"

"I can't move my legs. Where is this?"

"You're in the hospital, baby. There was an accident and your legs got hurt."

She lifted her head and looked at her legs and I saw the fear enter her eyes. Her chin started to quiver. "Daddy, I'm scared."

"No, no, sweet girl, you don't have to be scared. You're going to be okay. The doctor fixed your legs."

She looked at her legs again and bit her lower lip. "But I can't move them."

I wanted to take her in my arms and order the fear to leave her alone. That was my job as her daddy, to protect her, to ward off pain and uncertainty and fear. It was my solemn duty, my highest calling, and I'd failed at it. Instead I inched closer to her bed, lifted her head and slipped my arm under her neck. It was the best I could do next to scooping her up and rushing out of the hospital, taking her to someplace safe where little girls didn't lose their mommies and have their legs screwed back together again. But such a place didn't exist. "You will be able to as they get better."

Lizzy looked around the room, sleepy-eyed, and licked her lips. "Daddy, where's Mommy?"

My throat constricted as if two unseen hands had wrapped around it and squeezed. Tears immediately pushed on the back of my eyes. What was I to say? How could I tell this child—my child—that her mother was dead, that she'd never see her again, never sit on her lap or snuggle into her hug, never hear her read a bedtime story or say "I love you, pumpkin"? But I had to, I knew I did. I couldn't lie to her, tell her Mommy was just fine and she'd see her soon. I brought her hand to my mouth and kissed it. "Sweetie, there was an accident—"

"A car accident?"

"Yes."

"I don't remember it."

"I know you don't and that's okay." I caressed her cheek with the back of my fingers, thankful she had no memory of that awful event. "Listen to me, Lizzy, okay? Mommy ..." I couldn't do it. The tightness in my throat was too much, the lump that had lodged there was too big. I couldn't get words past it. Swallowing hard, I pushed back the tears that threatened to ruin the whole thing and just said it. "Baby, Mommy went to be with Jesus."

"You mean she died."

Lizzy was a smart girl and my best bet was just to shoot straight with her. I nodded as a tear snuck past the dam I had built and slid down my cheek. "Yeah, she did."

She paused and closed her eyes. After a few seconds, Lizzy's eyes opened and focused on me. "Will I ever see her again?"

"Sure you will. One day." My voice squeezed past taut vocal cords. "For now, though, we have lots of pictures at home and you have lots of memories. You can see her whenever you want."

She thought about that as tears built in her eyes. Her chin quivered again. Suddenly, panic took over her face. She looked around the room at the monitors and IV pole, at her legs, at me, then coughed out a sob. "I want Mommy here."

I stood and wrapped my arms around her, careful not to disturb her IV lines, and held my daughter as she cried into my shoulder. Anger came over me again like a summer thunderstorm, quick and violent. No seven-year-old should have to go through this. How would she ever recover? How could I soothe her pain? I was helpless and weak. My daughter, my Lizzy, was overcome with despair. There was a bully beating her and I could do nothing but stand by and offer empty platitudes. She was in the darkest place of her life, a valley most children never had to navigate.

And I blamed myself.

***

Word of our tragedy got around outside the hospital and by midafternoon visitors starting showing up, mostly those acquaintances from our previous church and a few of my clients. They filed in one by one, wore grim masks, and stood outside Lizzy's room and cried or said how sorry they were, asked if there was anything they could do. Yeah, bring my wife back and heal my daughter's legs. I hated it. They're all good people. Great, actually. And the very fact that they took time out of their day to check in on us meant a lot. But I was in no mood to talk or accept condolences or say thank you for the prayers. I just wanted to be alone with my daughter so we could grieve together.

Lizzy slept through most of it. In fact, the first three days in the hospital she slept most of the time. They had so much pain medication pumping through her system she could barely keep her eyes open long enough to eat a few bites of food. Also, I think on some deep, subconscious level, the sleep was her mind's way of not having to deal with the pain of the moment.

I know she dreamed of Annie while she slept because at times she'd cry her name or murmur under her breath. I'd never seen anyone cry in their sleep until I saw my Lizzy do it. It's a chilling thing to watch.

The most heart-aching was late one evening. She'd been moved to a private room on another floor and slept peacefully while I sat by her bed and watched over her. It was the least I could do. I was afraid to sleep, afraid she'd awaken in the middle of the night, frightened and alone. I'd failed in keeping her safe; I would not fail in keeping her company.

At a little before eleven, Tom knocked softly on the door of Lizzy's room. His large frame took up most of the doorway and blocked the hallway light from entering. He'd visited her every day at different times, I think as much to see me as her. He was the only visitor I looked forward to seeing. Tom had a mild, knowing demeanor that comforted and eased my distress. His deep voice was like a kind of relaxation therapy.

I waved him in and he shut the door behind him.

"How was Miss Lizzy's day?" he whispered. He'd started calling Lizzy "Miss Lizzy" almost immediately and I'd taken a liking to the name.

"Same," I said. "Sleep, eat, bathroom, sleep, a little TV, eat, sleep some more." I paused. "Still lots of crying."

Tom leaned over Lizzy's bed and rested his big hand on her arm. "Can't blame her for that."

"I don't."

"You blame yourself."

I didn't say anything. Tom lifted one of the other chairs in the room and set it next to mine alongside Lizzy's bed. "Ben, it ain't your fault what happened. You know that, don't you?"

Again, I said nothing. I didn't know it. As far as I was concerned, I was responsible for Lizzy's pain, for Annie's death. There was no one to blame but me.

"Jus' happened is all," he said, looking at Lizzy's legs. "Sometimes things happen without any kinda explanation."

"Like the fire."

Tom nodded slowly. "Yes, sir. Like the fire. I've gone over and over it a million times in my head how that fire started. It was in the basement, old wiring. I spent a good year blamin' myself, wishing I'd-a replaced those old wires, cleaned out the basement, anything. Connie and Jeffrey would still be here." His eyes misted.

I didn't know what to say. I could have told him it wasn't his fault, that it could happen to anyone. But then he'd tell me the same was true for me, what happened was not my fault. Only it was. I was convinced of it. "I'm sorry, Tom."

"Me too. Every day I'm sorry."

"Did you ever blame God?" I needed to know.

Tom pushed out his lower lip and shook his head. "Nope. Never blamed him. Asked him plenty a questions, pretty direct ones too. Did lots of cryin' and some hollerin'. But it wan't his fault the fire started. We live in a messed-up world and there's plenty of sufferin' to go around. Plenty, indeed."

I was about to say something when Lizzy stirred and tossed her head from side to side. She coughed once and rubbed her eye. "Mommy." Her voice was soft but urgent. "Mommy went to ... my mommy ... she ..." Her voice drifted off.

Tom shifted in his chair. "Is she awake?"

I kept my voice low, just above a whisper. "No. She's been doing this lately."

"Talking in her sleep?"

"Yeah. Most of the time it doesn't make any sense, just mumbles and nonsense stuff."

Lizzy coughed again. "She's not here anymore ... she ... where are you? Mommy?"

A single tear seeped from the corner of her closed eye and slipped down over her temple.

"Why did he take her?" Lizzy turned her head to face us and furrowed her brow. "I want ... I want ... Mommy."

I couldn't help it; I started to cry. I looked at Tom and he was crying too. Here we were, two grown men sitting in a darkened room listening to a little girl talking in her sleep and both crying like babies.

Eventually, Lizzy settled and fell silent again. I wiped my eyes and Tom wiped at his. He looked at his watch. "I gotta go. It's late." It was near midnight. He stood and replaced the chair on the other side of the room. As he walked by me he rested his hand on my shoulder. "You got a good girl there, Ben."

"The best. She's just like Annie in so many ways."

He squeezed my arm. "I'll see you tomorrow."

Annie's funeral. I needed to get home and make sure I had a shirt and pair of pants ironed. I also needed to shower and shave. "Thanks, Tom. I'm glad you'll be there."

"My prayers will be with you ... and Miss Lizzy always."

Lizzy wouldn't be going to the funeral. I hadn't even told her about it. I would someday when she asked.

CHAPTER 7

....

I DIDN'T WANT ANNIE'S FUNERAL to be a big deal. Not because she didn't deserve it; she did. If anyone deserved to be remembered and honored it was my Annie. I was in no mood to talk to other people, to endure their weepy condolences, their memories, their requests to help. I just didn't want to do it. I wanted to say goodbye to Annie by myself, just me and her. I wanted to cry in private, mourn with no one else around. Annie and I weren't big social butterflies, even when all was going well at the church. We'd enjoyed getting together with other couples on occasion but mostly we thrived on being alone as a family, taking picnic lunches to the state park, going on long walks in the woods, drives to see the fall foliage, going out for ice ...

I'd arranged it so the whole service would take place in the cemetery. Annie never liked funeral homes and she abhorred viewings; said they were creepy and awkward. And I knew that, despite my secret wishes, a lot of people would show up, so I wanted to make the farewell as simple as possible. Annie would have wanted that too.

When I arrived at the cemetery Tom was already there, dressed in a dark-blue suit, white shirt, blue tie. He looked every bit the preacher. He stood by the hearse talking to a minister he'd asked to perform the service. When he saw me, he smiled, and they both approached the car. Tom was the only person I didn't mind talking to.

I got out of the car and was hit by the heat of the morning. The sun was nearly at full strength and already it was nearing ninety degrees. Sweat beaded on my forehead and I loosened the tie around my neck.

Tom extended his hand. "Mornin', Ben. Fine day for a funeral. Jus' fine."

"Annie liked hot days," I said. "The hotter the better."

Tom motioned to the man by his side. "This is Reverend Charles James, a friend of mine from seminary days."

Pastor James shook my hand too. "It's a pleasure to meet you, Ben." He had warm brown eyes that offered compassion and wisdom and years of ministering to grieving people. "I'm so sorry about what's happened. How are you feeling this morning?"

I shrugged. "I don't know. I'm kind of numb, you know?"

He put his hand on my shoulder. "Don't fight it. It'll take some time for the feeling to come back in your life."

Tom nodded and gave a quiet "amen." "How's Miss Lizzy this mornin'?"

"She was still sleeping when I went by her room this morning. I told the nurse to tell her I'd be back after lunch and would spend the rest of the day there."

I took my seat under the tent they'd set up around the burial plot. Annie's casket was there, suspended over the hole in the ground that they did their best to conceal with green outdoor carpeting. Flowers adorned the top of the casket and the ground around the tent. Pastor James greeted people as they arrived and pointed them in the right direction. Some stopped by to shake my hand or give a hug and whisper how sorry they were into my ear. I knew most of them but a few I'd never seen before. They said they were friends of Annie from high school. I smiled politely and apologized for not remembering them.

A warm breeze moved through the tent and rustled the flowers, flapped the canvas awning. Someone behind me said it was the spirit of God making his presence known.

Annie's parents arrived, as did my mom. My dad, who'd suffered a stroke a few years back, was absentee. It was too much for my mom to transport him such a long distance.

The parents sat on either side of me. Both moms wept softly. Despite the fact that they'd driven all the way from North Carolina for the funeral, I wanted to stand up and shout at all of them, ask them where they'd been the past three days, the past twenty-nine years. I wanted to walk over to Annie's dad and tell him he had no right to mourn for the daughter he'd abused for so many years, then go to my mom and yell at her for allowing my drunk father to take his anger and frustration out on the both of us all those times.

Soon the service was underway. I looked around and found Tom standing in the back of the crowd, hands clasped in front of him, his head glistening like a polished bowling ball. He smiled and dipped his chin.

Pastor James began with the obligatory scripture reading from John 11. Jesus' words: I am the resurrection and the life ...

I didn't hear much more after that. My mind wandered and I found myself twenty years ago in North Carolina ...

***

I attended my first funeral when I was nine. My grandaddy died in February in the middle of a North Carolina ice storm. Heart attack. He was a farmer, a hard worker, and never saw a doctor a day in his life, except the day he was born. One day, at the age of fifty-seven, while he was feeding the cows, his heart just stopped. He lay there in the barn for a full ten hours before my grandma slipped on her thickest winter coat and braved the falling ice to look for him. She never talked much about it but did say that from the look frozen on his face she thought he'd been scared to death. I couldn't imagine what would frighten a man like my grandaddy that much.

He had it in his will that I'd be a pallbearer. I don't think he ever thought he'd die so young, never imagined he'd have a nine-year-old bearing the weight of his casket. So that's how I wound up standing alongside my dad and his three brothers and my great-uncle Booger, hefting Grandaddy's casket up a slippery hill in the middle of Mount Peace Cemetery.

The hill wasn't that high nor the slope that sharp, but with a half inch of ice covering everything it might as well have been Mt. Everest. About halfway up my Uncle Booger glanced back at me and said, "How you doin', kid." He always called me "kid" or "the kid." I don't think he ever even knew my real name.

I told him I was fine, and I was. He and my dad were toting the bulk of the weight on our side. I just offered a steadying hand and went along for the ride.

"Your grandaddy's a heavy bugger, ain't he?"

Uncle Booger was Grandaddy's older brother by ten years and he was the talkative one. My dad said he had diarrhea mouth; it just kept running and running.

I didn't say anything. He wasn't heavy to me. I looked back at my dad and saw the strain on his face. Not only was the casket heavy but finding your footing on the sloping ground was about as easy as catching a greased pig with your feet.

"I don't know what possessed him to buy a plot on top a hill," Booger said. "Maybe it was to keep folks from coming to see him, knowing they'd have to climb this thing to do it."

When we were almost to the top of the hill Booger's foot slipped and I had to sidestep quickly to keep from tripping over it. But the quick movement caused my own feet to slip on the ice and I lost my footing and went down. I slid back and took out my dad's legs. Grandaddy's casket hit the ground hard and shot like a sled down the hill. Dad cursed and Booger let out a yell, something I couldn't understand. One of Dad's brothers, Uncle Nathan, started to run after the casket, but he, too, lost his balance. His feet shot up in the air like someone had kicked them out from under him, and he landed on his butt and slid down the hill behind the casket, the tails of his jacket flapping in the breeze like a bird attempting liftoff. The casket made a straight line for the hearse, plowed into the side of it, popped up almost on end, and tipped to the side. The lid broke open and Grandaddy's lifeless body toppled out and onto the ice-covered grass. My mom and several of the other ladies present shrieked, Dad cursed again. Booger let out a howl that sounded a lot like a laugh.

I sat there stunned, cold, embarrassed, and horrified. Grandaddy was a big man, not huge, but big enough that the mortician had just cut his clothes and put them on his body from the front. Now, lying face down on the ice, Granddaddy's posterior lay exposed for all to see. The hearse driver and Pastor Withers did their best to roll Grandaddy over, and by the time they did my dad and his brothers were there to help put the body back in the casket.

After that I promised myself I'd never attend another funeral. Never. Little did I expect then that I'd be attending my wife's funeral at the age of twenty-nine.

***

A hand on my shoulder stirred me from the memory. Pastor James stood close. He was tall and built thick, like a retired football player, and had a smile that crinkled his eyes. "Ben, would you like to place the first flower on the casket?"

I stood and numbly went through the motions of laying a single rose on Annie's box. Tears pressed behind my eyes but I held them back. I knew once I let them come they would flow hard and heavy and there was no telling for how long. And I didn't want to make a scene here. Annie's mom followed with a flower, then my mom. Pastor James said a short prayer and then it was over. Again, people filed by me, hugging, crying, whispering apologies, condolences. I never heard most of them. I just forced a smile and nodded and held back those tears.

When the crowd had thinned, I found Tom by his car and headed that way, but someone caught my eye before I could reach him. A woman, standing some thirty feet away. Young and attractive. I stared at her for a moment, my heart stuck in my mouth. It was Annie, only it wasn't. It was Becky, her sister, come all the way from California for the funeral. I never really knew Becky and only had one real conversation with her. That was at our wedding, right before she ran off to California to flee her parents and the South and all the bad memories.

Our eyes met. I smiled and nodded, but couldn't turn away. She looked so much like Annie, more so than I remembered. She couldn't have known it, but she had the exact same hair color and style as Annie, as if they'd gone to the same stylist on the same day. She had the same eyes too, and cheekbones and mouth. They could pass for twins.

Finally, I turned to leave, but she stopped me. "Wait. Ben."

I turned and faced her. Becky stood before me and if I hadn't known better I'd-a thought it was Annie come back from the dead for one more goodbye, one more "I love you, Benjamin Flurry," one more hug.

"Hey." It was all she said. She looked nervous and her eyes were red-rimmed and swollen from crying.

"Hi Becky. Thanks for coming such a long way."

She smiled and my tears almost made it past the levy I'd built. "It wasn't so far."

That's exactly what Annie would have said. "I didn't mean the miles."

"Neither did I." She paused, glanced back at the casket, wiped tears from her eyes. "I never told her that when I left, went to California, I was running away from our parents, that house, North Carolina, all of it, but I never ran away from her."

I couldn't help it; a single tear slipped past the dam and puddled in my eye. I quickly dashed it away and swallowed hard. "I think she knew."

Becky smiled again and nodded. "Good." She reached out and took my hand. It felt just like holding Annie's again. "How's Lizzy?"

"The surgeon says she'll walk again."

"But how is she?"

Like my Annie, Becky was a thinker and she wasn't content with small talk. "Right now, she's handling things exactly how I would expect her to. Lots of tears, little talk, sleeps a lot. She's strong, though, like Annie. Probably stronger than me."

"Annie was always the stronger of us too. Do you mind if I stop by and see Lizzy?"

"Not at all. She'd like that. Annie talked about you a lot."

Becky's eyebrows arched. "She did?"

"She never stopped looking up to you."

"And I thought I was the one who looked up to her."

I told her how to get to the hospital and where to find Lizzy's room, then left. At the car Tom said, "You okay?"

I nodded, looked back at Becky. "Yeah. I just need some time alone."

Tom moved his chin toward Becky. "Who's that?"

"Becky. Annie's older sister. I haven't seen her in six years. She's the spitting image of Annie. It's uncanny."

Tom smiled. "Ben, Annie was a beautiful lady."

I opened the car door. "You have no idea."

CHAPTER 8

A T OUR HOUSE, I parked my truck in the driveway, got out and started walking, didn't even go inside. I needed the fresh air and open space. I crossed the backyard and hit the cornfield at almost a run. The tears came then, fast and fierce, and blurred the world before me. I didn't care, though, and made no attempt to wipe them away. In a way, they seemed liberating, as if they could wash away the hurt and pain and loneliness and anger. Like that dirty river water that washed away my sins all those years ago, the tears cleansed me from the inside out.

It took me only a matter of minutes to cross the field and reach the tree line. There I stopped and rested my hand on a thick-trunked sycamore. The smooth bark had peeled off in large sections, revealing the mottled white wood beneath. Above, the tree's sprawling branches and large, palmate leaves spread a canopy over me that blocked the sun's light. More tears came and my knees buckled. I sat on the ground and let the sobs purify my pain.

I had no idea how much time passed before I ran out of tears and sat there panting like a man who'd just run a marathon. Standing, I ran my hand over the sycamore's trunk, knocking off a large section of bark. Annie loved this tree; she was fascinated by the bark, said it reminded her of the way sunburnt skin peels, which reminded her of our honeymoon to the North Carolina shore. I got burnt real bad there. Five-alarm bad. My skin peeled for weeks.

***

We went to Ocracoke Island. Nothing extravagant. It was no Tahiti or Bermuda, there was no crystal-clear, blue Caribbean water, no fancy wet bars along the surf, no swimming with dolphins. Just us and the surf and the salt air. And it was paradise. Our first day there we unloaded the luggage from the car and stuck it in the small cottage we'd rented for the week, then headed for the beach. It was only a block from the house, which was situated along an uninhabited stretch of shoreline. A thin sheet of sand covered the roads and sidewalks. There were a few other homes dotting the landscape, but mostly our neighbors were clumps of woody seashore elder shrubs, beachgrass, and dunes. We held hands and walked in the surf. It was early November and the water was just starting to turn cold. Overhead, the sky was low with a blanket of ashen clouds. A steady wind blew south to north and whipped Annie's hair around her face.

She closed her eyes and walked by just the feel of my hand in hers.

"You ever think of being a parent?" She had a slight smile on her face.

"We just got married," I said. "Let's not rush things."

She opened her eyes and nudged me. "I'm not talking about that. I mean do you ever wonder what kind of parent you'll be?"

"Honestly?"

"No, lie to me. Start our marriage off the right way."

"I haven't given it a lot of thought."

She was quiet for a moment. I watched her walk, the wind against her face, the faded freckles dotting the bridge of her nose, her perfect lips and chin. It was the same face I'd studied most of my life, but somehow now it seemed different, or at least I looked at her in a different way. She was beautiful and I felt like the luckiest man on earth, maybe the luckiest to ever live.

"I have. I can't wait to be a mommy ..."

She left her sentence without a period.

"But ..." I said. I had an inkling where she was going with this, what was bothering her.

"But, well, both of us grew up in pretty dysfunctional families."

"You're too kind."

She nudged me again with her shoulder. "Be serious."

"Okay. Sorry."

She bit her lower lip. "I mean, I had a father who felt like a man by beating up on his children and a mother who couldn't have cared less. Not exactly good examples to follow. You had a dad with a big mouth and a mom scared to death of him. We don't come from very good stock."

"And you wonder if that will rub off on us. If in some way that rotten parent gene got passed down to us and no matter how hard we try we'll always default to being the parents our parents were."

She stopped and looked at me, then reached up and pulled my head lower and kissed me square on the lips. "Yes. Exactly."

I took both her hands. This was something that had bothered her for some time. "But that's not how it works, Annie. There is no bad parenting gene. Our folks had a choice to make and they made the wrong ones over and over again. But it was their choice. Don't soften what they did by making them victims. We have the same choice and we can choose to be good, loving parents. And we will. We'll spend time with our kids and talk to them and laugh at all their stupid jokes and they'll laugh at ours. We'll tuck them in at night and say prayers with them and eat meals as a family. We'll go on picnics together and walk beaches just like this as a family. And we'll never hit our kids in anger or belittle them with words. We can choose that."

She kissed me again, more passionately this time, then said, "I love you, Benjamin Flurry. You're just the man I need."

We went back to the cottage and spent time together as only a husband and wife should.

Our last day on Ocracoke, the sun shone brightly as if it were only a few thousand miles away. Annie and I spent the whole day on the beach, soaking in the rays, smelling the salty air, and listening to the rhythm of the ancient tides. I fell asleep more than once, the gentle, warm air caressing my face, the sound of the water's ebb and flow lulling me into peaceful, contented slumber.

When I awoke it was midafternoon and I suggested we take one last walk on the beach before we headed home the next day. I wanted to see the Ocracoke lighthouse. I slipped on my sneakers and took her hand. A quarter mile down the shore the pain hit me and I could barely walk. Despite my best effort to protect my fair skin from the sun's rays, I'd forgotten to put sun block on the tops of my feet. They'd lain exposed the entire day. I sat on the sand and grimaced as I slipped off my shoes.

Annie was by my side. "What's wrong?"

"My feet." They were rubbed raw by the sand in my sneakers and as red as tomatoes.

Annie's hand went to her mouth. "You didn't—"

"No, I didn't."

"How are you going to get back to the house?"

I shrugged. "I guess I'll have to walk unless you feel up to carrying me?"

It was no laughing matter but we both laughed anyway. I did make it back to the cottage and into the shower. The cool water felt good on my toasted skin. That night, I slept fitfully, suffering chills then sweats then chills again, and the next morning both my feet were the size of pineapples and now an awkward shade of purple. Annie drove us home as I sat in the passenger seat and moaned.

I never did find the lighthouse.

***

The sound of footsteps brought me back to the present. Turning, I found Tom, still in his shirt and tie, hands in his pockets.

He smiled and shrugged. "Thought you could use some company. You okay?"

I peeled off a section of bark, broke it in half, and held the pieces in each hand. "Annie loved these trees."

"Sycamores."

"Yeah. She was fascinated by the bark, said it reminded her of ..."

He waited for me to finish.

"I still can't believe she's gone. I can't believe that was her in that box we put in the ground today. I keep expecting her to walk through a doorway or to call me or to feel her touch first thing in the morning before I open my eyes."

I lifted my head and looked him right in the eyes. "Tom, I don't know what I'm going to do without her."

He didn't hesitate. "You're gonna mourn her absence and get on with life. You're gonna be the daddy Miss Lizzy needs. And you're gonna find you can't do any of it without God carryin' you."

"It feels like he's abandoned me."

He tilted his head sideways and met my eyes. "Do you really believe that? That he's abandoned you in your greatest time of need?"

I didn't. Of course I didn't. It went against everything I'd ever learned or experienced about God. I shook my head.

"The distance is created by you, son." Tom paused. He was slipping into his preacher mode. "I've found that there are two ways people react to suffering. They either run to God or run away from him. And right now you're puttin' more and more distance between you and him with each step. And that ain't what you want."

He was right, I knew he was, but he didn't know the whole story either. No one did. I didn't say anything. I couldn't.

Tom stepped closer and put a hand on my shoulder. "Son, there's two kinds of sufferin' we go through. Trials God allows and consequences we done brought on ourselves. This is a trial. You didn't cause this, it just happened. But what happens, see, is when folks go through a trial and run from God they start makin' poor choices and those consequences start showin' up and then start pilin' up. And before you know it, you're so buried in trouble you can't see the light no more." He squeezed my shoulder. "Ben, you gotta turn and head the other way. Run to him, fall into his arms, let him carry you through this."

They were good words and I knew Tom was sincere. But I just couldn't do what he asked of me. I couldn't do it. Not yet.

CHAPTER 9

I BROUGHT LIZZY HOME FROM the rehabilitation hospital on a Thursday. A steady rain had been falling since before the sun rose and the ground around our house was soaked and soggy. She'd been in the rehab hospital a total of two and a half weeks and had made good progress but still was unable to bear weight on her mending legs. The fixator was still in place and her left leg was still casted from ankle to hip. She had to sit longways in the back seat of the car because she couldn't bend her knees.

After shutting off the engine, I jumped out of the car, ran around to the trunk, and retrieved the wheelchair. It took me a good minute to get the thing unfolded and the leg rests situated so when Lizzy sat on it her legs stuck straight out like two tree limbs. By the time I got the chair ready I was nearly soaked through to my skin. I lifted Lizzy carefully from the seat, one arm under her legs, one under her back, and set her in the wheelchair.

My plan had always been to bypass the three steps to the front porch and wheel the chair around to the back of the house where the patio was level with the back door. Only the ground was so saturated and soft now that the chair's wheels kept getting stuck. It was time for plan B but I didn't have a plan B. If I had been thinking straight (which I hadn't been since that awful night) I would have spent the last two weeks building a ramp to the front porch.

I had to improvise.

"I'm sorry, baby," I said, as I left Lizzy sitting in the chilly rain so I could make a dash for the front door and prop it open.

When everything was ready, I scooped Lizzy from the chair, careful to support her legs, and carried her up the steps and into the house. I wanted to avoid this route because every motion, subtle or not, caused jolts of pain to shoot up my daughter's legs. She'd been through enough pain and I didn't want to cause her any more. Once inside I sat her on the sofa, propped her legs with pillows, and returned for the wheelchair.

Leaving the chair on the porch, dripping water from every corner and joint, I went inside to find Lizzy on the sofa in tears. It had been a long day for both of us, a long drive home, and a rough walk to the sofa. I'd hurt her, I knew I had.

Kneeling beside the sofa, I handed her a tissue and stroked her hair. "Baby, I'm so sorry. I'm so sorry. How are your legs?"

More tears came. "They hurt, Daddy."

"I know." She just had her pain pills before leaving the rehab center so I couldn't give her any more for another three hours. "I'm sorry." It was all I could say. Again, that feeling of utter helplessness was there and I hated it, loathed it. I was her daddy, her protector, the one who fixed everything and made the boo-boos feel better. But now I could do nothing but kneel there and apologize and let my little girl hurt. "Is there anything I can do for your legs? More pillows? Less?"

She shook her head and wiped at her tears. "I just want Mommy." She was too young to have to go through something like this. Right there I wanted to scream at God, ask him how he could let a precious child like Lizzy suffer this way. Where was the mercy we heard so much about? In my heart I railed and thrashed, shot questions heavenward like machine gun fire.

Lizzy must have seen my inward battle in the lines of my face. She put her little hand on mine but said nothing. It was the exact thing Annie would have done. Even at seven years old she was so much like her mother. Her touch was enough, it always had been.

"Baby, we'll get through this. I promise you we will."

"How? Without Mommy?"

Now tears pressed on my eyes. Lizzy was smart enough to figure out that soon I'd have to return to work. My supervisor had allowed me to take the rest of my vacation time, which amounted to a week and a half and then an additional four weeks, two with pay, two without. That meant I had one more week at home, one week to figure out how Lizzy and I would do on our own without the glue that used to hold everything to-gether. "I really don't know, but we will. We'll figure it out."

She turned her head and gazed out the window, her eyes misty and distant. I could see the fear in them, the uncertainty, the pain, and it tore at my heart.

I leaned over and kissed her forehead. "You want to sit by the back door and watch the rain fall?" Lizzy used to love to watch the rain fall. On warm summer days we'd even sit out in it, see who could last the longest with the rain pummeling our faces. Lizzy always won.

She dropped her eyes and shook her head.

"C'mon, you love watching the rain come down." I nudged her arm. "I'll even wheel you out there so you can sit on the patio like we do."

She glanced at me and a slight smile curled the corner of her mouth. "Not in my wheelchair."

"Why not?"

"Dad, 'cause it'll get all wet."

"It's already wet. It'll be okay."

She thought about it, which surprised me, then said, "I think I'll just sit by the back door."

"Inside or out?"

She almost smiled again. "Inside, silly."

"Okay, okay. I'll stop bugging you."

I retrieved the chair and wiped the water from it then lifted Lizzy and set her in the seat, her legs propped on the leg rests. Pillows were stuffed around her to pad her legs and arms. "Comfy?"

She nodded.

I wheeled the chair over to the glass doors and parked Lizzy where she could get a good view of the back yard. The rain still fell steadily, heavier now than when we arrived home, and puddled on the lawn. The sky was a flat gray, the color of old concrete, and the world around was wet and filled with muted colors.

"You okay here?" I said. I had second thoughts about sitting her in front of something so depressing. "You could watch some TV, a movie or something."

"No, this is fine." Her eyes were motionless, fixated on the rain. I think in some strange way the blandness of the scene was exactly what she needed to calm her nerves and lull her into a comfortable mood.

"Would you like some apple juice?"

She didn't pull her eyes from the glass. "Yes, please."

I rubbed her head. "Thank you for the good manners."

In the kitchen, I poured two cups of apple juice and stopped at the counter to sip mine and watch Lizzy. She sat statue-still in that chair, transfixed on the outside world. The swelling had come down a lot in her right leg but it was still so discolored and battered. I wondered how she'd ever walk on it. I wondered how I'd care for her. How I'd manage going back to work. I wondered what would become of us without Annie around. And suddenly fear overcame me, doubt rose up like a geyser and spilled forth question after question. Questions I had no answers for. Tears sprang to my eyes.

Setting the cups on the counter, I went to the sink and splashed water on my face. I had to get a grip, be strong for Lizzy. Without Annie to anchor her life, I was it, and if I crumbled she'd be lost.

After drying my face with the dish towel, I returned to the counter. Lizzy slumped to one side and her head rested on her shoulder. She'd fallen asleep to the even rhythm of the rain. It was just what she needed. The image came back to me, of standing by that door, an infant Lizzy in my arms, and watching a storm front come in.

The storm was upon us now.

Our family had been disrupted and joy was a thing of the past, a thing of memories and snapshots. A chill started at the base of my skull and tingled down my spine.

What was I to do? How could I introduce Lizzy to happiness again when I was so sad? How could I pull our little family together when I was so broken? How could I be her daddy when I didn't even feel like a man?

I downed both cups of juice, lay on the sofa next to Lizzy, and soon fell into a restless sleep.

CHAPTER 10

I HATED THE NICU AND its rows of beds protected by clear plastic shields. Its monitors and their constant beeps and chirps. The steady hum of the ventilators. But mostly I hated the feeling that permeated the place. It was saturated with despair and heartbreak. Here was where parents came to visit their newborns, the baby girl or boy they dreamed of taking home and swaddling in a soft blanket and rocking to sleep. They no doubt had the nursery decorated and ready to go, diapers purchased, outfits sorted and folded neatly in drawers. But here lay their precious ones, some barely larger than a man's hand, kept alive by machines, clinging to life.

I hated it.

I kept thinking my daughter didn't belong there. She'd be fine. Just let us take her home. But the neonatologist insisted our little Lizzy stay for observation. She'd gone without oxygen for too long in the birth canal and they wanted to make sure her brain was functioning as it should before they released her. Three days tops, that's what he told us.

Every day I'd roll Annie in her wheelchair to the NICU to visit Lizzy. Our baby was one of the largest in the unit and didn't have much of the tubing and sensors a lot of the preemies had. We were the lucky parents, the ones who got to feel their daughter's skin, even hold her. She was only there to be monitored, not kept alive with a thread's chance of ever going home.

At least that's how we should have felt, but every day Annie would stroke Lizzy's soft skin and ask me, "Do you think we'll be able to take her home?"

I knew her question was more loaded than it sounded. She wondered if Lizzy would develop like other kids, "normal" kids. If she'd walk and run and jump. If she'd go to school and learn her times tables and memorize the Gettysburg Address.

And every day I'd lay my arm across Annie's shoulders and kiss her hair and answer, "Yes. She's going to sleep in her crib in her own room and learn to walk on our floor and play games in our backyard. She'll bring her homework to us for help and put on silly skits and memorize every line of *Anne of Green Gables* so she can recite the entire movie with you. She'll ask a million questions about a million different things and one day she'll smart-mouth us and be proud of herself for doing it. That's when the real work will begin. She'll grow into a smart, beautiful young lady and take after her smart, beautiful mother in every way possible. At least I hope she will."

On the third day, Annie sat in the rocker in the NICU and rocked Lizzy. The doctor told us we'd be taking her home later, he just needed to complete the appropriate paperwork and fill out the discharge instructions. Lizzy slept in Annie's arms, her eyelids resting perfectly on chubby cheeks. Wisps of dark hair dusted her head and her lips puckered involuntarily. As far as anyone could tell, she was perfect. She'd passed all the doctor's tests; her reflexes were normal; brain function, normal.

But Annie seemed uneasy. She kept running her finger over Lizzy's nose, stroking it slowly from between her eyebrows, down the bridge to the tip. Across the room, a couple stood holding each other. The woman, a slender girl who looked like she hadn't slept in weeks, cried quietly. The man beside her held her in his arms, his chin resting on the top of her head. Their baby lay motionless under its plastic canopy. A nurse put her hand on the woman's arm and reached up and turned the monitor off. Another win for hopelessness.

Annie turned her head and looked at me, tears in her eyes. I knew what she was going to say before she said it. "That won't be us, will it?"

I put my finger in Lizzy's hand and kept my voice low. "Absolutely not. We're going home today. Lizzy is fine."

"But what if something happens? I keep feeling like something's going to happen, like we're never going to make it out of here. Like—"

"Annie, stop. Nothing is going to happen."

Annie looked around the room. "I wish the doctor would hurry up."

"Easy, babe. Don't worry about a thing."

Eventually a nurse came to us with a folder and a sheet of paper we had to sign. Finally, we were free to go. We put Lizzy in her car seat and I got the car while an elderly gentleman wheeled Annie and Lizzy to the patient pick-up area. Annie sat in the back seat with Lizzy. Before pulling away from the curb, I reached behind me and took Annie's hand in mine, found her in the rearview mirror. "Honey, we're a family now. Nothing is going to change that. I won't let anything happen to Lizzy. Okay?"

She stroked Lizzy's cheek and nodded.

***

I awoke with my head in a dense fog, disoriented, confused. I'd slept soundly. It took me a few seconds to get my bearings. I was on the sofa in the living room, it was raining when I fell asleep, Lizzy had fallen asleep in her wheelchair by the door looking out over the backyard and the field. Only now Lizzy wasn't there, nor was her wheelchair.

Panic seized and tightened my chest. I sat on the edge of the sofa and wiped the remnants of sleep from my face. Had I moved her before lying down? No, I hadn't. I'd left her right where she was because she was sleeping. I thought I'd only sleep a few minutes. A quick glance at my watch told me I'd been out for nearly two hours. Maybe she'd moved herself. She'd propelled the chair enough times in the rehab center. But that was in the therapy gym where there was lots of room to maneuver. I doubted she could navigate the furniture and tight spaces of our house by herself. She would have made noise and awakened me.

I stood, still confused, and put my hands on my hips. Unease banged away at my rib cage. "Lizzy?"

I searched the kitchen, the small dining area, and the living room. All were empty. The second floor was out of the question. There was no way she folded her wheelchair and carried it up the steps while scooting up on her bottom. Back to the family room I went. It had stopped raining outside, and a few scattered rays of sun had pushed through the cloud cover. That's when I noticed the sliding glass door was unlocked. Not wanting to think the worst, pushing even the hint of that thought from my mind, I quick-stepped to the door and scanned the outside.

Lizzy was there, in her chair, Tom seated beside her. They both faced the field and watched a doe and her fawn pick at the corn left by the harvester. Exhaling a slow breath, I slid the door open and stepped outside.

Lizzy swung her head around first.

"Hi, Dad. You're awake."

The rain had brought a drop in temperature, making the hairs on my arm stand on end.

Tom stood and stuck out his hand. "Afternoon, Ben. Jus' stopped by to see how Miss Lizzy was doin'."

"We didn't want to wake you, so Mr. Tom rolled me out here to talk."

My first intuition was to scold both of them. Lizzy for leaving the house without telling me and Tom for sneaking around taking people's children from their homes. But it sounded a lot worse than it was and Lizzy needed a friend like Tom. We both needed a friend like Tom.

I shook Tom's hand and smiled. "Thanks for stopping by. Sorry I was sleeping so soundly." He'd stopped by the rehab hospital almost every day to see Lizzy and talk with me. Over the past few weeks he'd become a good friend and consistent fixture in both our lives.

Tom brushed off my apology. "You need your sleep too, son. Get it where you can. Me and Miss Lizzy was having a good talk, ain't that right Miss Lizzy."

I kissed Lizzy on the head. "Can I get you a blanket or something if you're going to stay out here? It's getting chilly."

She crossed her arms and hugged herself. "Sure."

Tom patted my shoulder. "I'll get it. I have to use the men's room anyway."

"Thanks. There's a blanket on the back of the sofa in the family room. Bathroom is to your left on the other side of the kitchen."

Tom walked away and I sat next to Lizzy. "So what were you and Mr. Tom talking about?"

The doe and her fawn were still out there, surely aware of our presence but not letting it spook them away from their midafternoon meal. Lizzy watched them intently. "He was telling me about his son, Jeffrey, and the fun things they used to do together."

"Really? Like what?" Tom had never opened up to me about the relationship he'd had with his son. I knew he loved the boy dearly but that was it.

"They used to go fishing together a lot. Mr. Tom said he was teaching him how to fly fish when Jeffrey ..."

She let her words hang but I knew how they ended: when Jeffrey died. She couldn't bring herself to say the word.

"They also loved to rock climb. They'd go in late fall when the snakes are all gone—Mr. Tom hates snakes—and they'd spend all day climbing rocks and exploring different places."

She paused and bit on her lower lip.

"What is it, Lizzy?"

She looked at me and there was a sense of deep hurt, of lostness, in her eyes. "Dad, did Mr. Tom tell you how his wife and Jeffrey ..."

"How they died?"

She nodded.

"Yeah, he did."

"When he told me I wanted to hug him."

For seven years old, Lizzy showed an incredible ability to empathize, to set aside her own pain and comfort someone else in theirs.

"You should have."

"I couldn't from this chair."

She returned to watching the deer. Another doe had joined them. This one was a little more skittish and kept lifting her head to look in the direction of the house.

"Did you know Mr. Tom used to read to Jeffrey every night?"

I stroked her hair. "No, I didn't know that." I knew where she was going with this.

"Just like Mommy used to do with me. He said they were reading *Treasure Island*."

Annie and Lizzy were working their way through *Anne of Green Gables* for the second time. "She loved reading to you. And I used to love to listen to her read to you."

"I miss her. Sometimes I think she's still here and will come get me, or I think I hear her laughing. Is that weird?"

I knelt on the wet patio and wrapped my arms around my daughter. She hugged me back. "Absolutely not. It's the way it should be."

The glass door slid open and Tom emerged carrying the blanket. "Here ya go, Miss Lizzy." He unfolded it and spread it over Lizzy's legs.

She grabbed the edge and pulled it to her chin. "Thank you, Mr. Tom. And thank you for coming by and telling me about Jeffrey."

Tom shot me a glance then smiled at Lizzy. "You're welcome. I was having a gloomy day so thought I'd come by and let you brighten it."

She smiled again. "The rain stopped just when you got here."

"It was that sunshine coming outta your face that chased it away. Hey, do you mind if me and your daddy go for a little walk, just out in the yard."

Lizzy shrugged. "I don't care."

Tom looked at me and nodded. "You okay with that, Ben?"

"Sure. You okay there, Lizzy? Are you warm enough?"

"Yes, Daddy. I'm fine."

Tom patted her head. "We won't be out of sight."

"You need anything you just say so, okay?" I said.

She nodded. "Mmmhmm."

Tom and I walked out into the wet grass. It hadn't been cut in weeks and was up to our ankles. My sneakers got wetter with each step. I didn't care. I was glad for the time with another man, a man who understood what it was we were going through.

"How you doin' with things, son?"

As we grew nearer to the edge of the property, all three deer lifted their head and stared at us, ears perked.

I sighed. "I don't know. At times I think I'm coping, getting along okay, then something will happen or Lizzy will say something that reminds me of some specific thing Annie did or said and I get lost in that dark place again. I still cry myself to sleep every night."

Tom was quiet for a few seconds. The deer jerked and bolted away, bounding like springs across the field, changing direction every few feet. "I cried myself to sleep for six months." We stopped walking and he faced me. "I hate to say this 'cause of the way it sounds, but at first you'll think about her all the time, every second of every day."

"I do. I can't get her out of my mind nor do I want to. Sometimes it's as if she's still alive and has just been gone on vacation or something. I think she'll come back any day and walk back into our lives."

"Time will pass, though, and you'll find yourself still thinkin' about her every day but not all the time like you do now. There'll be times when you get busy doin' something and realize you haven't been thinkin' about her. And you'll feel guilty about it."

Tears were building in his eyes. His wounds, though years old, had never fully healed. I wondered if that kind of wound ever did heal completely and scar over.

"After a while you won't feel guilty about it no more. You'll understand it's a part of the healin' process and it's okay not to think about them every second of the day."

He'd gone from *her* to *them*. He was talking to himself now.

"They tell me the day will come when you don't think about them every day. Life will go on and their memory will fade. Days may go by before something triggers a memory." He paused, wiped at a tear and sniffed. "I haven't gotten there yet."

I didn't want to get there. I never wanted my memories of Annie to fade. She was too much a part of me. It'd be like forgetting my own name. I turned my face to the house and saw Lizzy sitting in her chair, blanket to her chin. I couldn't forget Annie as long as our daughter was around. She was too much like her mother.

CHAPTER 11

DURING THE NEXT WEEK, Tom and I built a ramp from the sidewalk to the front porch. We were heading into the rainy season and I didn't want any more replays of leaving Lizzy out in the rain while I propped the door open and carried her up the steps. Tom did more of the work than I did. He was a whiz with his hands, like he was born with a hammer and saw in each. I was good at measuring and holding boards in place, that was about it.

When the last nail was hammered, Tom raised his thick hand above his head, hammer grasped in his fist, and smiled. "Wanta try it out?"

I clapped him on the back. "Thanks, Tom. No way I could have done this without you."

"Sure you could have." He smiled big, showing his pearly teeth. "Little determination, you can do anything you put your mind to."

I jumped on the ramp, testing its sturdiness. It didn't budge or sag. "Well, maybe I could have built it, but using it would be another story."

Tom tossed the hammer on the ground and propped his hands on his hips. He nodded toward the house. "Go get Miss Lizzy and let's see how it does."

I stuck my hand out and Tom took it in his. "Thanks, Tom. I mean that. You've been a good friend to us. I was serious when I said I couldn't have done this without you."

"Aw, don't think nothin' of it."

"No, I think a lot of it. I think a lot of you." And I did. Tom was a good man, probably the best I'd ever known. And knowing what he'd been through, the valleys he'd traversed in his own life, the storms he'd endured, made his selflessness all the more impressive and moving. He'd found a way to take the focus off of himself and cast it on to others. He'd moved past the pain and found his way out of the darkness.

Still holding onto my hand, Tom cocked his head and lowered his eyebrows. "What is it, son? What's got you all sentimental?"

I looked at the ramp. "This for one. I never thought I'd be building a ramp for my daughter, you know? Kind of bittersweet, finishing it."

He patted my hand then let go. "It's more than just a bunch of wood and nails, isn't it?"

"It's a new way of life, at least for a while." The surgeon said Lizzy may not walk for another month and most likely wouldn't be doing steps before Thanksgiving. The ramp would get a lot of use.

I sat on the ramp and pulled my feet up so my knees almost touched my chin. On the other side of the street, Mr. Boyd pushed his mower across his lawn, making a checkerboard pattern. "I go back to work in a couple days too."

Tom sat on the steps next to the ramp but didn't say anything. He knew when to speak and when nothing needed to be said. I surmised his years of pastoring and counseling taught him that.

"Ms. Connors is a good woman. I'm not nervous about her staying with Lizzy. That's not it at all." Judith Connors was a middle-aged widow at our former church who had volunteered to sit with Lizzy and keep up with housework when I went back to work. She insisted up front that I not try to pay her and said even if I tried she'd refuse. She said her late husband left her enough insurance money to fund a small country and she had nothing to do all day but busy herself around the house and garden.

"I know that's not it," Tom said. He watched Mr. Boyd lay down that perfect grid in his grass. "You don't want to leave Lizzy. You lost Annie and you're afraid if you leave Lizzy you'll lose her too."

It was as if he had some x-ray vision into my head and read my thoughts as easily as if they were printed in black and white.

"What if something happens?" I said. "What if she needs me and I'm not there for her?"

"You've lost control, haven't you?"

I didn't answer his question. I knew where he was going with this. Mr. Boyd shut off his mower and retrieved the edger from his porch. He plugged it in, turned it on, and ran it in a straight line where lawn met sidewalk.

"You know, no matter how hard we try or how tightly we hold on to things, we never have control in the first place. Not really. We think we do. We think we can order life—" He pointed at Mr. Boyd. "Keep our rows straight and edges clean. But, really, all we're doing is trying to keep up with the ever-changingness of life." He looked at me and put his hand on my knee. "There's only one who is truly in control."

Still, I said nothing. I knew what he said was the truth. In my heart I knew it, but my head didn't want to accept it. I could have prevented that car accident, that was within my control; I was certain of that.

"You need to trust him, son. He's got Lizzy in his hands."

I wanted to say, "Like he had Annie in his hands? Really? You expect me to buy that?" But I didn't. I was in no mood for an argument. I didn't have Tom's faith. Maybe at one time I did, but it had since been bruised and broken. I didn't know if it would ever be the same again, if it would ever be whole.

Tom stood. "He doesn't have to earn your trust, son. It's already due him." He stepped up onto the porch. "Now I'm gonna get Miss Lizzy and see how this here ramp works."

He left me sitting there with my battered faith and wounded pride. I'd been a Christian long enough that I knew I couldn't argue with him. He was right. I was wrong. I got it.

It just hurt that I trusted the ramp he'd built more than I trusted God.

CHAPTER 12

WHEN I LANDED MY first job with the Department of Environmental Protection, I thought I'd won the lottery. It was my first full-time job and the first one I'd interviewed for. I'd had part-time jobs here and there during high school and summers. Landscaping, dock work at the local Piggly Wiggly, even did time at a few different fast food joints. Whatever I needed to do to make a few bucks and buy gas for my pickup. But the job at the DEP beat it all. It was a real job with real pay and real benefits. State benefits. State retirement if I stayed on long enough.

I found out I'd won the job over seventy-some other applicants. For some reason they liked my personality, thought I was a good match for the department. I called Annie right away and told her. She said she was coming to Pennsylvania so we could celebrate properly. The next day she arrived at nine in the morning and knocked on the door of my apartment. She'd driven all night to greet me with a hug and a half-empty can of Mountain Dew. I brought her inside and insisted she sleep at least a few hours. If we were going to celebrate properly, I didn't want her falling asleep on me.

It didn't take Annie long to fall asleep. I gave her my bed and went for a jog while she rested. When I came back, I showered, dressed, and stood in the doorway of my bedroom watching the girl of my dreams, my best friend, the only person in the world who truly knew and understood me, sleep. She'd only been in Pennsylvania two hours and I didn't want her to leave, didn't want her to go back to North Carolina. She belonged with me; it was fate or God's will or whatever you wanted to call it.

Around noon, Annie stirred and woke up. Her hair was pressed to one side like a fancy Sunday hat and she had pillow creases across her cheek.

She'd slept soundly. After showering and doing all the things women do to make themselves presentable, she emerged from the bathroom and smiled. "Are you ready to hit the town?"

My apartment was in the village of Ramblewood, population right around a thousand. Ramblewood has three streets and one neighborhood. There is no town to hit. Fortunately, State College is just a few miles north and, being a college town, it has plenty of eateries and places to celebrate a new job. And to be in love.

I grabbed the keys to my truck. "What are you in the mood for?"

She didn't hesitate. "Pizza."

Annie was always in the mood for pizza. Any kind. Didn't matter the topping. She liked it all.

I gave her a sideways look. "I'm thinking something a little more so-phisticated for such a special occasion."

"So what do you have in mind, smart-pants?"

"How about Thai?" I threw it out there not knowing if she'd bite or not. Boomer was not known for its cultural diversity. A Thai restaurant there would be about as out of place as a polar bear in the middle of the Sahara.

Annie walked to me and put her arms around my waist. "Wherever you want to go. It's your job and your celebration."

I kissed her gently. "Nope. It's *our* celebration."

We did eat Thai and Annie loved it. After the meal, I drove us to an overlook in the Rothrock State Forest, atop Stone Mountain. We got out of my truck and leaned against the front bumper, shoulder to shoulder. Before us stretched miles of deciduous forest sprinkled with dark patches of pines. For several minutes neither of us said anything; we were content just to be together. From our vantage point, the sky formed an endless ceiling dotted with picture-like cumulus clouds. The terrain below sloped down into a valley then rose on the other side like a green wave frozen in mid-swell.

I put my arm around Annie's waist.

She rested her head on my shoulder and sighed. There are different kinds of sighs, one of frustration and exasperation, one of deep thought, one of fatigue, and one of contentment. I've learned to tell the difference, and her sigh was definitely one of contentment.

"So how do you feel about the job, really?" she finally said.

"Nervous and excited."

"Why nervous?"

I shrugged. "I feel like there's a lot riding on this, like I have everything to prove and I better not ruin it."

Annie lifted her head and looked at me. "Who do you have to prove something to? Not me. I believe in you, Benjamin Flurry."

I kissed her forehead. "You always know the right thing to say."

"I mean it too."

"Thanks." I paused, watched a hawk light from the top of a pine and glide in a wide arc above the valley below. Her question weighed on me, sat on my shoulders like a backpack full of rocks. Who did I have to prove something to? "My parents for one. My dad. He told me my whole life I wouldn't amount to anything more than a grunt, like him. He told me to forget about college, that it was a lot of money wasted on some piece of paper that didn't mean squat. That I could be working instead of burying my nose in books, making real money and earning a real living."

"Your father didn't know what he was talking about, Ben, you know that."

She was right, I did know it, but it didn't take the sting out of his words.

"And myself," I said. "I need to prove to myself that I can do this, that I can hold down a real job, one I'll support my wife and children with, one I'll build a career out of and hopefully retire from."

"That's quite a tall order for your first job."

Again, and as usual, she was right. I was putting a lot of expectations on one job and one man working that job.

She put her head back on my shoulder and took my hand in hers. "Maybe you should just take it one step at a time."

"And what's the first step?"

"Starting the job. You may get there and hate it, quit in a week."

"Not hardly. I'm going to give it everything I have."

"Because that's the kind of man you are. You're not a quitter." Her faith in me was humbling. How could I not love her and want to spend the rest of my life with her?

"And what's the second step?"

"Getting married."

I drew in a deep breath of the cool mountain air. The scent of leaves and pine was in the air. "I'd like to get married someday, but I have to find the right girl. I'm pretty picky, you know. She has to be really special to meet my standards."

"Do you have anyone in mind?"

"Well, there's this one girl, a real Southern belle, charming, smart, funny. And I think she loves me."

"Do I know her?"

"You might. She's from Boomer, North Carolina, a hole-in-the-wall town that people say nothing good has ever come out of, but she wasn't born there so I guess they can't be talking about her."

Annie lifted her head from my shoulder and stood in front of me. She looked me right in the eyes and I found tears in hers. "I know that girl," she said, her voice quivering. "And she loves you with all her heart."

"And how do you know that?"

"She told me so. She tells me every minute of every day. She wants to marry you."

My hands took to sweating and my heart started pounding a steady but quick rhythm in my chest. I could feel my pulse all the way to my fingertips. "Annie Fleming, will you marry me?"

Tears pushed out of her eyes and trickled down her cheeks. "Yes, of course I will. Of course I will."

"I don't have a ring to give you. Not right now anyway."

She kissed me squarely on the lips. "I don't need a ring. I've been dreaming about this day since we were thirteen. All I need is your promise."

"I do promise," I said. "I promise to love you and marry you and have children with you and grow old with you. I promise to give you everything you need and protect you. And I promise to never lay a hand on you

out of anger. Annie, you have to know that. I will never hit you. Never."
I knew she needed to hear that. She was a strong person, the strongest
I ever knew, but she was still a person and had fears and anxieties, and I
knew no matter how much her heart told her I wasn't that kind of person,
wasn't like her father, her head told her the possibility was still there, that
people change, sometimes for the worse.

She kissed me again, so lightly I hardly felt her lips on mine. "Thank
you. I believe you."

I held her face in both my hands. Tears still ran from her eyes. "I'll
never let anything or anyone hurt you, you hear? I promise that."

Whether I realized it at the time and just didn't want to acknowledge
it or not, I don't remember. But somewhere deep inside I had to know I
was making a promise I could never keep.

CHAPTER 13

MY FIRST DAY BACK at work started off rather uneventfully, just like I'd hoped it would. I left Lizzy with Ms. Connors and a paper full of instructions covering everything from how to wheel the chair down the ramp, to how to lift Lizzy without disturbing the external fixator, to how much and when to give her the pain pills. Ms. Connors assured me she and Lizzy would be just fine, that she'd raised three boys of her own and dealt with broken limbs on a semi-regular basis. I felt compelled to remind her that none of them were as broken as Lizzy's, though. She agreed and patted me on the arm, a motherly gesture that told me to leave, Lizzy would be just fine in her care.

My first stop of the day was the Martin farm. I was a DEP farmland inspector. It was my job to visit farms on a regular basis and make sure they had workable manure and pesticide management and disposal plans. I'd inspect where they stored their manure and how they managed to dispose of it and how they used and disposed of the pesticides they used on their crops. Before landing my job with the DEP I had no idea folks made a full-time living inspecting other folks' manure piles. Not the most glamorous job, I'll admit, but for me it was prestigious in its own way.

I had fifteen farms I inspected and worked with to make sure they were up to date on all the new regulations being passed down by the Environmental Protection Agency on the federal level. My mind was a virtual encyclopedia of every chapter, code, and act on the books.

Over the years I'd worked with my farmers, I wouldn't say we'd become friends but they surely didn't loathe my visits. I was not a brutal inspector writing up fines and leveling threats. My desire was to see every farm in compliance so they could stay off the radar of those above me on the bureaucratic food chain. I took the time to talk with them and get to know them on more than a business level. Take, for instance, Bill Martin, an honest man if I'd ever known one. He was the son of a farmer and married Loretta, the daughter of a farmer. Dirt and corn and livestock were in his blood. Bill and Loretta had two daughters and a son. Both daughters were in college and Caleb, their son, was a senior in high school. Next year they'd have three college loans to pay off. The last thing they needed was the state leveling fines on them or the feds paying them a visit. Last year I spent considerable time helping them completely rewrite their manure management plan so that it came within compliance of the latest regs and codes.

Bill saw my truck coming and met me in front of the barn. He was right there when I climbed out, extending his hand. "Good to see you back on the job, Ben. I heard about what happened." He put his hand on my shoulder and squeezed. "I know sorry doesn't mean anything but I am. The wife and I've been praying for you, praying hard. How's your daughter?"

For some reason I glanced at my watch. Lizzy had been alone with Ms. Connors for just over an hour and I wondered how they were making out. "She's coming along. Should be getting the external fixator off next week."

Bill stood in front of me and kept his hand on my shoulder. His eyes were deep set and crystal blue. Crow's feet radiated out from the corners, cut deep by too many hours squinting into the afternoon sun. In those eyes I found sincerity and concern. "I mean how is she really doing?"

I nodded slowly. "As good as can be expected, and I'm not expecting much. She has moments when she still cries a lot, talks in her sleep, that kind of stuff."

Bill clapped me on the shoulder. "Is there anything we can do?"

That he would even offer showed the caliber of a man Bill Martin was. "That's nice of you, Bill, but I can't think of anything offhand."

"If anything comes up you let us know, okay?"

I didn't say anything, partly because our relationship was through business and I didn't want to give even the perception of imposing on him or his wife beyond those boundaries, and partly because I wasn't sure if he was serious or saying what others thought was the proper thing to say to someone who'd been knocked down and beaten up by life.

But Bill wasn't the kind of man to say anything unless he meant it. He tilted his head and found my eyes. "Okay?"

I nodded. "Yes. Thank you. Now, how about we get to business."

I was halfway through the inspection and ankle-deep in manure when Loretta Martin came running into the barn red-faced and out of breath. "Ben, your sitter is on the phone. She needs to talk to you now."

Slipping off the rubber boots now sticky with manure, I made a dash for the house. The Martins weren't primitive folk but they kept things simple. Their only phone was a wall-mounted rotary job with a spiral cord. I found it resting on the kitchen counter and put it to my ear. "Hello?"

"Ben." It was Ms. Connors.

"Is everything all right? Is Lizzy okay?" I could only imagine what had happened. She'd fallen and knocked the fixator loose or lost control of the wheelchair and toppled it.

"She's not hurt but she's hysterical. Ben, she wants you to come home. She keeps saying she's afraid she'll never see you again." I could hear the panic in Ms. Connors' voice. She was a competent woman but there were some things even the most qualified of people couldn't handle. A hysterical seven-year-old was one of them.

"Put her on the phone, please."

There was a moment of silence then Lizzy's small, quivering voice. "Daddy?"

"Yes, baby, it's me. What's wrong?"

Loretta Martin stood in the doorway of the kitchen, her back to me, head bowed. I didn't mind that she heard my end of the conversation. She was a mother and knew some of what I was dealing with.

"Daddy, I want you to come home. Come home now, please." Her voice was stretched thin with panic and tears.

I wanted to reach through the phone and take my daughter in my arms, stroke her hair, tell her I was okay and would be okay. At that moment, I hated my job because it was the thing that took me away from Lizzy, separated me from her and stood between us like an uncrossable chasm.

I could have done what some parents might do, probably what parenting books would have told me to do: tell her she needed to calm herself and be strong for Daddy, that I'd be home when my work day was finished and until then she would have to dry her tears and be a big girl for Ms. Connors. But I didn't care what others would do or what some book recommended. My pain was as real as hers. "Baby, I'm coming home. I'll be home real soon. I love you."

I hung up the phone and stood there, arms crossed, leaning against the Martins' kitchen counter.

Loretta turned around and gave me a knowing look. "You're doing the right thing, Ben. She needs her daddy more than you need to inspect our pile of poop."

Thirty minutes later I arrived home. Lizzy and Ms. Connors were waiting for me on the front porch. As soon as she saw me, Lizzy started crying again. Her eyes were red and puffy.

Ms. Connors met me at the top of the stairs. She kept her voice low. "She's been inconsolable, so worried you wouldn't make it home."

"I'm sorry, Ms. Connors," I said. "I guess it was too early to leave her. Thank you for your help."

That evening I sat on the sofa with Lizzy's head in my lap, a mug of Earl Grey in my hand. We'd propped her legs with pillows and gotten her real comfortable. Her eyes closed and opened slowly as she wrestled back the sleep she needed.

With my other hand I stroked her hair. "Go to sleep, sweetheart. You need your sleep."

"I'm afraid, Daddy."

"Why?"

"Every time I sleep I have scary dreams." She paused, closed her eyes slowly then opened them. Sooner or later she would have to give in. "I see bright lights and hear the crash. Mommy screams. Then everything gets dark but the noises are still there."

Tears pressed behind my eyes. Normally when Lizzy had bad dreams Annie would sing to her, something soft and sweet, and that would put her back to sleep. I was no singer and didn't know any songs. "Things will get better, sweetie. They will. Just try to go to sleep now. I'll sit here with you."

"I love you, Daddy."

"I love you too, little buddy. I love you."

Her eyes drifted shut and this time did not open again.

I sat there until after midnight, when Tom got off, thinking and planning, weighing my options and the pros and cons of each. I still had some money in the savings and the check from Annie's life insurance had come in the mail a few days ago. I could afford to take more time off work, but not much more.

At 12:30 I picked up the cordless phone and dialed in Tom's number. He picked up on the second ring.

"Hello, Ben."

"How'd you know it was me?"

"Who else would be callin' me at this hour? Besides, I'd been wondering how the day went."

"Not well." I told him everything and he could no doubt hear the pain in my voice.

"What do you wanta do?"

"I have to do something radical. We need a change of scenery, a change of life. And I need help with Lizzy. Full-time help."

"What's your plan, son?"

"To move back to Boomer. It's crazy but it's a good town, slow-paced, quiet, just what we need right now. And there's a good hospital close by for Lizzy. Good schools too. I don't know what else to do."

He was quiet for several long seconds. Finally, "I think you're doin' the right thing. Where you gonna live?"

"With my parents until the house here sells. Then we'll get our own place down there. I know it's crazy, believe me I do. But since my dad's stroke, he's stopped drinking and can't talk anyway. All he does is sit in his wheelchair and watch TV all day. And Mom was a nurse, she'll know how to care for Lizzy. She'll love her too."

Another pause on his end, then, "Ben, I been thinkin' 'bout some-thing for a while now and prayin' 'bout it, and I think I just got my answer. I want to help you out."

"How?"

"Look, I got my house all paid for and everything and it's just me, you know? I want to take care of your mortgage until the house sells. It'll be one less burden on you and give you time to find a job down south."

Again the tears pushed on the back of my eyes. "You don't have to do that."

"I know I don't have to. I want to. I'll miss having you two around."

"We'll miss you too. You've been a true friend to us. You're more than welcome to come to North Carolina anytime you want."

He sniffed. "I might just take you up on that. That'd be real fine."

I clicked off the phone and tossed it on the coffee table, took a sip of tea. I wasn't sure I was doing the right thing for either Lizzy or myself, but I needed to do something and it sounded like a good plan. We both needed a new start and I'd find the help I needed with Lizzy in my mom. I didn't feel like I was going home again. Home was where Annie was. Since she'd passed, I'd been without a home, wandering aimlessly, trying to make sense of life, bring back some order, some normalcy. But so far I'd failed. Even our own house, with all the memories and pictures and smells, seemed foreign and out of place.

The one thing that bothered me and twisted my gut was leaving the cemetery where Annie was buried. I knew that wasn't her in that box in the ground, that she was in heaven having the time of her life, but it would help Lizzy's recovery and healing if there was a physical place she could visit and remember her mother. I knew she wouldn't want to leave as long as Annie's burial place was still here. My only solution was to move the body to a cemetery in Boomer, the place Annie grew up and we fell in love. It seemed fitting. And I would have put money on the fact that Annie's parents would pay for the relocation.

CHAPTER 14

WE LEFT OUR HOME in Pennsylvania two weeks later, driving my SUV and hauling a trailer packed with everything we owned. It took us that long to sell most of the furniture, put our house on the market, and arrange for an orthopedic surgeon to continue Lizzy's care in Boomer. I wanted the transition to be as seamless as possible for Lizzy, both physically and emotionally. She'd taken the news of our move pretty well. As I'd anticipated, her only concern was where Annie would be buried. She wanted her mommy close to wherever we lived.

Moving Annie's casket wasn't cheap, but I was able to persuade her parents to cover the cost and coordinate the arrangements. They found her a nice plot in Boomer Gardens.

We arrived at my parents' home on a Tuesday evening, just before sunset. My mother was there to greet us on the porch. She came down the steps wearing her apron—the same one she'd had since I was a kid—and wrapped her arms around me.

"Boy is it good to have you home again, Ben." She cupped my face in her hands and smiled, tears in her eyes. "This is your home, it always was. I want you to be comfortable here."

Then, leaving me, she hurried around the front of the vehicle and opened the passenger-side rear door. "Well look at you," she said as she took Lizzy's hands in hers. "You're so big and so pretty. My, you look just like your momma."

To say my mother's behavior was normal would be to say it was perfectly common to see gators sprout wings and fly in a V formation. This was not the mother I left eleven years ago. She'd spent thirty-one years taking verbal punches from my dad on a regular basis. She'd learned to retreat into a safe place, somewhere deep within herself, and hide her true feelings, her wants and desires. They didn't matter anyway, at least not to the man to whom she'd promised her faithfulness. He only cared about himself and his booze. And she knew her place.

But here she was anyway, Miss Congeniality, doting on her grand-daughter.

"C'mon, Ben, let's get Lizzy out of here and get her into the house."

I did as she asked and scooped Lizzy into my arms, supporting her legs. She'd gotten the external fixator removed a week before and now wore long pants.

"Take her inside," my mother said. "You can put her on the sofa. It's soft and comfortable. I'll start unloading the car."

I stopped and faced her. "Where's Dad?"

She looked at me, glanced away, then back at me. "He's in the den watching TV. It's all he does anymore. Sit in that chair and watch TV."

I started to walk away but her hand on my arm stopped me. "He's not the same, Ben. He's not the same man he was when you left for college. Since the stroke ... he's changed."

"I know, expressive aphasia." He couldn't berate her with words any-more, not any of us.

"That's not what I mean. He's different, in here." She pointed to her heart.

"Different? How?"

She glanced at Lizzy then at me. "He's got Jesus now."

"How do you know? He can't talk to tell you."

"I can tell. I've been his wife for going on thirty-three years. I can tell he's different. Jesus has changed him."

All I could think of was Pastor Flowers standing at the front of that tent begging people to come forward, give their life to Jesus, and my dad standing stone still, dead in every way but physically. He went to the meetings for show, so the rest of Boomer would see him there, not be-cause he felt he needed any of it. For the millionth time I second-guessed my decision to bring Lizzy to this house.

My mom smiled at me and again the tears were in her eyes. She nodded and bit her lower lip. "He's told me in his own way. You'll see. There's a gentleness about him now."

As much as I disbelieved the whole thing, it certainly explained the change in Mom's demeanor. She no longer felt threatened, beat down, disregarded. She could be herself, find the woman who had been hiding for three decades. She now enjoyed life and it showed, radiated from her.

I dipped my chin and kissed Lizzy on the forehead. "Okay. Let me put Lizzy inside and I'll be right out to help you."

In the living room, I put Lizzy on the sofa and kissed her again.

"Daddy?"

"Yeah, baby."

"Are you happy we came here?"

I paused and ran a hand over her hair. "Yeah. I think we're doing the right thing. You remember what I told you about Granddad, though, right?"

"That he has trouble talking?"

"Yeah."

"I remember."

"Just be patient with him, okay?"

"Daddy?"

"Yes?"

"Is Granddad nice?"

The man I remembered was anything but nice. But if what my mother told me was true and he was a changed man ... I could only trust her. "Yes. I think he is."

"Good."

I ruffled her hair. "Yeah, it's good. I'm gonna help Grandma unload the car. You okay here by yourself?"

"Yes."

The sun set fast and soon it was time to put Lizzy to bed. I was to stay in my old bedroom and Lizzy would get the spare room across the hall. Mom had decorated it with pink walls and a Disney princess bedspread. But somehow Lizzy wound up in my room dozing in my old bed and I was stuck on the floor with a sleeping bag. I stayed with her until she fell asleep then snuck downstairs and sat on the porch. Not much had changed in the house. Much of the furniture was the same and it still carried the musky aroma of old wood and frying oil.

The rocker was the same too. My dad used to sit in it every evening and smoke his pipe like he was king of the world or something, looking over his kingdom. Mom said he'd given that up too—both the smoking and the rocking—since his big change.

The night was cool and the crickets loud. A loose cloud cover let enough moonlight through to dust the front yard in a bluish haze. I shut my eyes and tilted my head until it rested on the back of the rocker. The sound of the runners on the wooden planks brought back all kinds of memories. Some of them good. I thought of Annie and how as kids we'd stay out late into the summer night, chasing fireflies and smelling the burning tobacco in my dad's pipe. She was always quicker than I was. I used to love how the moonlight glistened on her hair ...

To my left I heard footsteps in the grass and lifted my head. A figure approached the porch, a woman, silhouetted by the porch light of the Fleming house. For a moment, before my rational side could tell me it was impossible, I thought it was Annie. The moonlight in her hair. The curves of her shoulders and hips. The cadence of her gait.

The figure drew closer, teasing my senses, tricking my eyes. I was just about to say Annie's name when the woman stepped into the light and I saw her face. It was Becky, Annie's sister.

"I thought you'd be out here," she said. She rested her arms on the porch railing. "Mind if I join you?"

"Uh, yeah, sure. I thought you went back to California?"

She climbed the stairs and sat on the porch boards, her back to the railing. "I was going to but, well, let's just say I tried the whole California thing and it didn't work out."

"So you came back here?"

"Crazy, huh? I guess I needed someplace familiar to regroup after ... you know."

She meant after Annie's death. "Yeah, I know."

"And then I heard you were coming back to stay with your folks and thought I'd hang around, see if I fit in anyplace in Lizzy's life."

"You're her aunt and my sister-in-law. As long as you're not a bad influence you have a place in both our lives."

She smiled. "Good. I'm looking forward to getting to know her. She seems like a great kid."

"She's the best."

"If she's anything like Annie."

"She's totally like Annie."

Becky drew in a deep breath and tilted her head skyward. "How are you two holding up?"

"We have each other. Right now that's enough. Soon things will change. Lizzy needs to get back in school and I need to find a job. But we both need some time to adjust first."

"I miss her," she said, and I could hear the tension in her throat. "I miss the kid who used to run around the yard screaming and laughing, the kid who still smiled regardless of the junk life threw at her. Her laugh. Her smile. The way she fixed her hair. The smell of her sweat. I miss it all."

Tears pushed out of my eyes and ran down my cheeks. That was my Annie. Becky and I were joined in our pain, companions in grief. We shared many of the same memories.

Becky wiped her eyes, then her nose, with her sleeve as she stood. "Man, I didn't mean to be all gloomy. Sorry." She put her hands in her pockets, arms stiff, the same way Annie used to when she felt awkward. "Hey, I better go before we both start a bawlfest. I just wanted to say hi and welcome you back home."

I looked past her into the moonlit yard, the grass, the trees, the shrubs, all powdered with a lunar glow. "I'm not home, Becky. I'm a million miles from home."

CHAPTER 15

MY DAD AND I only had one conversation that I can remember. He was a man of very few words, except when he was using them to bully and manipulate. His words were his weapons and came in spurts, like bullets from a machine gun. Normally my father didn't talk *with* someone, he either talked *to* them or *over* them, and sometimes right through them. And he couldn't have cared less if anyone actually listened to him, he talked more to hear himself speak than to be heard. His voice was big and boomed like cannon fire and he liked to talk loud and overpower you with sheer volume. I think whoever coined the phrase *blowhard* had Walter Flurry in mind.

I was seventeen and feeling more like a man every day. I had ideas and dreams, opinions about everything from politics to sports to the environment. And I was itching to spread my wings and fly my father's coop. I'd applied to four different colleges: the University of North Carolina, North Carolina State, Virginia Tech, and Penn State. My first choice was Penn State because their environmental science program was second to none, so when the acceptance letter came I couldn't wait to show my parents. Maybe then my dad would show even an inkling of pride in me. Maybe then he would see me as the man I'd become.

All day I sat on that letter, waiting for Dad to come home from the warehouse, eat dinner, watch the evening news, and retire on the front porch with his favorite pipe. I pushed through the screen door and took the rocker next to him, the one he'd bought for my mom the year before. The one she never sat in because she could take neither his silence nor his sharp words.

Without saying a word, I handed Dad the acceptance letter. He took it and held it at an angle so the light from the window could illuminate it. I held my breath while his eyes scanned the letter, reading every word. When he finished, he folded it along its creases and handed it back to me, keeping his eyes on the darkened yard beyond the porch. He puffed on his pipe and continued rocking in silence.

"Well," I said. "Aren't you gonna say anything?"

He shrugged. "Ain't nothin' to say. So you're goin' to college."

"Penn State. It's a good school."

He snorted as if he knew anything about colleges, about which ones were good and which ones were a waste of time and money. "It's in Pennsylvania. What's the matter with the local schools?"

"Nothing. I applied to them and will probably get accepted too. But I like Penn State; they have a great environmental science program. This is the one I was really hoping to get into."

Looking back on that conversation, I should have just dropped it there. He wasn't interested, plain and simple. But at the time I couldn't see that, or didn't want to. I wanted him to be proud of me for something, to tell me I'd done a good job and he and my mom would be rooting for me. I needed him to accept me just this once.

Instead he blew out a thick column of smoke and said, "And what are you gonna do with that?"

"Lots of things. I could go into forestry or environmental protection or agriculture. It's what I'm interested in."

He was quiet for a while, sucking on that pipe of his and rocking back and forth, back and forth, until the sound of the rocker on the porch boards grew irritating. Finally, he shrugged and sighed. "You know your mother and I can't pay for it, dontcha? You're on your own there."

I expected that comment and was prepared for it. "I know. I got a good scholarship and they have a work study program where you work on campus to help pay for your tuition. I've already applied for grants and loans too."

"So let me get this right." He drew on his pipe and exhaled a puff of white smoke. "You're gonna spend four years of your life and more money than this house is worth to be a glorified farmer."

Frustration overcame me and wouldn't let me quit. He had to understand what an accomplishment this was. I had to show him.

"Dad, it's a college education, a degree. There's lots of things I can do with it. I can get some really good jobs."

"Oh, so already you're gettin' all high and mighty, like workin' at a warehouse ain't good enough for you. I provide for my family, don't I?"

"Of course you do, that's not—"

"We have cars that work, food on our table, clothes on our back."

"Yes, we do, but—"

He turned in his rocker and pointed his pipe at me. "I've made a good living down at the warehouse and I never spent a penny on college."

I sat back exasperated and hurt. Once again he'd managed to make it about him. I should have known better than to bring it up. I should have just waited for the day to come, packed my bags, and left without so much as a goodbye.

"Do you know how much a hardworkin' fork operator can make durin' the four years you'll be stickin' your nose in books, listenin' to other people tellin' you what to think?"

"I have no idea."

"You have no idea." He turned his face from me. "Good golly, I raised a genius." He waved his pipe around. "Go do what you want, get your piece of paper, find your dream job. Best of luck to you."

As quietly as I'd sat down, I got up, went inside and up to my room. There I tore the letter into a hundred pieces and littered the floor with it.

***

I awoke the morning after arriving at my parents with an uneasy feeling in my chest. I'd dreamed of Annie, of our honeymoon, that walk on the beach. Lying there, staring at the ceiling like I'd done how many hundreds, thousands of times as a kid, I listened to the familiar sounds of my parents' home. Not much had changed since the last time I lay in that bed. Mom was downstairs making breakfast. Pots rattled, utensils clinked. The smell of coffee and bacon wafted up to me. They'd changed the room and I was glad for that. It would have been creepy to re-inhabit the room after eleven years and find it hadn't changed since I was a teen. The walls had been painted, the carpet changed. And all new furniture made it a guest room no one had slept in. My parents rarely had guests. At least not invited guests.

I rolled to my side and sat up. Lizzy was not in the bed. I listened but didn't hear her voice on the first floor. She couldn't have awakened before me and walked downstairs. She would have fallen out of bed and landed on top of me. I was pretty sure that would have stirred me from my dream.

Mom must have carried her downstairs. But I couldn't picture my mother carrying Lizzy and wasn't comfortable with her navigating the steps with my daughter in her arms.

I got up and, after a quick stop in the bathroom, went downstairs. The aroma of cooking breakfast grew stronger the closer I got to the kitchen. My stomach grumbled.

In the kitchen, I found Mom in front of the stove, but no Lizzy. "Good morning, hon." Mom smiled at me and turned back to the stove where she was flipping bacon in a bath of sizzling grease.

"Morning. Where's Lizzy?"

Mom motioned with her head toward the door that led to the basement. "With your father."

Despite the fact that I wasn't happy with Lizzy being alone with my dad, I again wondered how my mother had moved Lizzy from floor to floor. "How'd she get down there?"

"I carried her."

She said it like she was telling me she dressed herself in the morning and I shouldn't be surprised one bit about it.

"Mom, I—"

"Now, don't you lecture me, Benjamin. I worked at the nursing home for ten years. I used to move grown men five times Lizzy's weight. I know what I'm doing."

"But you didn't carry them up and down the steps."

She looked at me with wide eyes, spatula hovering above the frying pan. "Well of course I didn't. Don't be silly. But Lizzy can't weigh more than fifty pounds. She's such a little thing. Stop your frettin'."

I stood in the middle of the kitchen, hands on my hips, not quite knowing what to say next, so I ran my hand through my hair and stared at the basement door.

"Well, go on down," Mom said. "We refinished the den. You should see it. Your father loves it."

I walked to the doorway and stood there, my feet glued to the linoleum. That uneasy feeling was in my chest again and I remembered what it was: the feeling I used to get every time I was around my father. My heart rate increased steadily and my breathing grew shallow.

Mom's hand found my shoulder and startled me. "Benjamin, he's not the same man. Go find out for yourself."

I took it one step at a time, slowly, as if the stairs were covered in ice and descended into a frozen subterranean cavern. Halfway down I heard Lizzy's voice and stopped. She was talking, but I couldn't make out what she was saying. Step by step I crept down the stairs until I could peek around the corner and see the whole den. It did look nice. Whoever they'd hired had done a good job. In the far corner, the familiar form of my dad sat in a recliner. From what Mom had told me, he could walk as long as someone held both his hands and, even with that, his gait was clumsy and unsteady. She said that despite his physical deficits and aphasia his mind was clear and sharp. Which, Mom said, probably made things worse for him. He had no way of expressing himself. Beside his chair was Lizzy in her wheelchair. Mom must have carried it down first, then Lizzy.

Lizzy reached out and touched my dad's big hand. "Are you scared?"

It was an odd question to ask a man who had never shown fear in his life, at least not in *my* lifetime. He had only invoked fear in others.

Dad paused, looked at Lizzy and nodded.

Lizzy patted his hand. "It's okay to be scared, Grandpa. I get scared a lot."

Dad glanced at her legs. "Um ... uh, you ... sh-shirt, no ... translate, um, no." He pointed to the wheelchair. "You ... go."

"I know what you mean," Lizzy said. "Someday I'll walk again. I know. But that's not all that scares me. My mommy's gone and it's just me and Daddy now and I don't know if he knows how to take care of me like Mommy did. And then I'll have to start in a new school soon and that scares me too. What if the other kids laugh at me?"

A knot settled in my throat. I had no idea my daughter had such fears. I'd been so busy trying to normalize our lives and take care of details related to the move and make the transition as smooth as possible that I'd totally overlooked the emotional needs of my seven-year-old girl.

I needed Annie.

Dad took Lizzy's hand in his and rubbed it tenderly, there wasn't even a shadow of hardness in his face. "You, uh, son ... better." He shook his head. "No, um ... learn ... Monday. No."

Lizzy waited patiently for him to finish, holding his hand the whole time. Finally, Dad gave up, sighed and shook his head.

"I'm sorry, Grandpa. I wish I could understand what you were saying."

He smiled at her and nodded slowly.

Lizzy leaned in and got as close to him as she could. "I wish I could have known you my whole life."

In the dim light of the den, I saw a single tear spill from my father's eye and run down his creviced cheek. He smiled, blinked, and shook his head. I'd kept Lizzy from him because of his temper, his harsh way with words. I didn't want to expose her to the man I'd spent the better part of my life with. I couldn't risk it. He had to know that.

He tapped his chest with his forefinger. "I do ... um ... turkey, no ... break my ..."

"It's okay, Grandpa," Lizzy said. "You don't have to say anything."

He nodded. "Yes. I want to ... cards, no ... need June, pen." He stopped and rubbed his face, obviously frustrated. As little as I cared for the man, I couldn't help but feel sorry for him. He was a prisoner inside his own body.

I'd had enough and rounded the corner. "Hey, sweetie, good morning."

Lizzy looked up. "Good morning, Daddy. Grandma carried me down here. She's really strong."

I kissed her on the forehead. "I guess she is, huh?" I said, then I nodded at my father. "Hey, Dad."

He looked up at me and I found in his eyes a tenderness I'd never seen before. Sorrow even. He smiled at me and offered his hand. I put mine in his and he squeezed, not hard, but firm, a good shake, man to man. He nodded. There were tears in his eyes and his cheeks were still wet. Finally he let go and looked away.

"Okay, Lizzy girl, breakfast is ready. How 'bout I carry you upstairs?"

"It smells good."

"Yeah, Grandma always makes up a good breakfast."

She turned to my father. "Will you come up and eat with us?"

"Honey," I said. "I think Grandpa likes to eat down here in his chair."

"Then can I eat down here with him?"

There was a moment of awkward silence. I was hesitant to let her spend too much time with my dad, partly because I still didn't trust him—eighteen years of abuse isn't erased so easily—and partly because I didn't want him to be able to just waltz back into my life and act like none of the abuse ever took place. It did and I remembered all too well. Even if he had changed, if he was a different man like my mom had said. Even if he'd found Jesus and it had softened his heart. And even if he wouldn't say a cross word now if he could, it didn't change the past. In my mind he had a price to pay for how he'd treated us and he wasn't slipping out of the noose so easily.

"No, I don't think so, baby. I want you to eat in the kitchen with me and Grandma."

She didn't like that answer but I wasn't going to change my mind. I glanced at my dad. "You can visit Grandpa again later. Maybe this afternoon. Okay?"

"Okay. Bye, Grandpa."

Dad smiled and nodded. "Uh ... Liz-zy."

***

After breakfast Mom cleared the plates from the table and put them in the dishwasher. She brought a dishcloth to the table and ran it over the smooth surface. When she'd finished she put a hand on my shoulder. "Can I talk to you for a minute?"

"Sure. Lizzy, stay here, okay?"

"Okay, Dad."

Mom handed her a towel. "Here, baby, maybe you can wipe the table down, just as far as you can reach."

Mom took me into the living room and wrung the dishcloth in her hands. "Ben, I probably shouldn't have but I listened to the conversation you had with Lizzy in the basement."

"Mom—"

"Wait. Let me finish. I'm sorry for eavesdropping. I am. But, Ben, don't use Lizzy to punish your father."

I opened my mouth but she held up a finger. "Wait 'til I'm done. He loves her, you know. And he loves you. He may not have shown it to either of us when you were growing up and he's so sorry for that. But he's ready to now. When Annie died he cried for days, kept saying Lizzy's name. Hers is the only name he says, did you know that? He can't even say my name. Calls me 'um.'" She put her hand on my arm and squeezed. "Ben, if he could talk he'd beg you to forgive him."

"I can't, Mom. Not so quickly anyway. I spent eighteen years living with his anger and attitude, being pressed under his thumb. This house was filled with tension and heartache because of him. It's a miracle I didn't wind up just like him. I can't just erase that and act like it never happened. It did."

"And you feel like you're the one to punish him for it, is that it?"

"No. I don't know. Maybe."

She let her hand slip from my arm. "Ben, I can't change the past and neither can your father. If we could we'd bring Annie back, believe that. And I know there's a whole life your father would change. All we have is what's in front of us. I want you to think about two things. Are you doing the right thing? And what kind of example are you setting for your daughter?"

She walked away and left me standing in the middle of the living room with a wounded ego. I knew she was right; there was no need to lie to myself. But my heart couldn't let go of the past so casually. I'd been wronged. Big time. And I wouldn't simply turn the other way and act like it never happened.

CHAPTER 16

THE WEEKS WENT BY and with each passing phase of the moon Lizzy grew stronger. A few weeks before Thanksgiving, she took her first steps with the aid of a walker. But the trauma to her legs had left her with a very noticeable hitch in her gait, one that slowed her down and sometimes pushed her off balance. She had to be careful and take it slow, a difficult task for a seven-year-old who'd been sitting in a chair for two months.

Eventually the day came when it was time for Lizzy to go back to school. She'd be attending Boomer Elementary and walk the same halls I had walked as a child. The night before the big day, I knelt on the floor next to her bed and stroked her hair.

"You ready for tomorrow?" I asked, knowing the answer. I hated that she had to go to Boomer El. It wasn't what Annie and I had decided on, but I needed to look for a job and the local private schools were much too expensive.

She bit her lower lip and shrugged. "I guess."

"You guess? You don't sound real sure about it."

"I'm scared."

I took her little hand in mine. "What are you scared about?"

She looked me right in the eyes and in hers I saw fear and uncertainty. "What if the other kids laugh at me because of my walker?"

"Oh, honey." I kissed her hand. "They won't. They'll love you. You're fun to be around and funny and smart. You'll get along just fine."

"But how do you know?"

And that was the question, wasn't it? How *did* I know? Truth was, I didn't. What I did know was how mean and ruthless children could be to one another. I'd been on the receiving end of their heartlessness more times than I cared to recount. It's never easy to send your daughter, your baby girl, into a pack of wolves, and part of me wanted to tell her right then that she didn't have to go, we'd find another way. But sooner or later she had to get back to school and I had to get back to work. Our savings was running dangerously low.

I swallowed and patted her hand. "You know what? You just be yourself, be Lizzy Flurry, and see what happens. My bet is that you'll be a real hit because the Lizzy Flurry I know is sweet and kind and friendly, the kind of girl who makes friends easily."

She shifted her eyes away from me. "You have to say that, Dad."

"Why?"

"'Cause you're my dad."

She had a point, but in my heart I believed every word I'd said, of course I did. If only the other kids would give her a chance, look past the obvious difference and get to know her.

"That's right," I said. "I am your dad and I love you no matter what."

Lizzy sighed deeply, dramatically, and stared at her hands. "I wish Mommy was here."

Unbidden, tears sprang to my eyes and that familiar lump was in my throat. I'd been waiting for her to say something like that and thought I'd be prepared for it. I wasn't. I tried to talk, to say anything, but the words wouldn't come. All I could do was take her in my arms.

"I miss her, Daddy. Why can't she be here?"

Finally, I found my voice. "I don't know, baby. I don't know. I miss her too."

We held each other for a long time, daddy and daughter, understanding each other's grief but not being able to do anything about it. I wanted to believe that death had robbed us both of something very precious and wounded us deeply. But guilt stabbed at me and scraped away at that open sore. Had we been robbed? Or was I responsible for Annie's death? Had I quickened death's hand? Those were the questions that haunted me in the night, visited me in my restless sleep and whispered condemnations in my ear. If Lizzy knew the truth of the matter ...

"Daddy," Lizzy said. "Will you pray with me?"

I slowly closed my eyes and opened them again, sighing deeply. I hadn't prayed since learning of Annie's death. I'd done plenty of questioning, plenty of hollering and even pleading. I'd thrown myself against the gates of heaven, pounded them with my fists, and kicked at them, even thrown curses their way. But really praying, having a sincere heart-to-heart with God, wasn't something I was interested in.

"You know what, baby girl? I think God would rather hear from you than me. He likes hearing from little girls."

"Okay." She paused and snuggled her face into my shirt. "God, I'm scared about tomorrow and I miss my mommy. I know she can't come back—" Her voice tightened and tears pushed out of my eyes. I held her tighter. "—so please tell her I love her and Daddy does too. We both miss her. Take good care of her too. And please help the other kids to like me and not laugh at the way I walk. Amen."

I said nothing. There wasn't anything to be said. Shame and hurt overwhelmed me like a tsunami making landfall. I should be able to pray with and for my daughter. I should be able to ease her fears and wipe away her tears. That was my job as her daddy. But I was too broken to lead her, to take her hand and guide her through this valley.

I did something then that I hadn't done in two months; I talked to God. I didn't holler, didn't accuse, didn't bargain or plead. My request was simple but heartfelt. *God, help me.*

Lizzy eventually fell asleep in my arms and, after laying her down and pulling the blanket to her shoulders, I took my place on the floor beside her bed and lay awake all night thinking of Annie and Lizzy and the family we used to have.

***

As a kid, I stuttered. It made me an easy target. Differences will do that. I have no idea why I stuttered or when it all started. Maybe it was some malformation of my vocal cords or a tripped wire in my brain, or maybe it was a glitch in my early childhood development brought on by the ever-present stress that permeated my home. Whatever the cause, I didn't stutter at all when I was around Annie, and by the time I got to high school it all but vanished. I believe to this day it was Annie's doing. She had that effect on me.

My stuttering was worst around my dad. I was an embarrassment. He saw my impediment as a sign of weakness and indecision and swore I'd never amount to anything if I didn't learn how to express myself. But the more he told me to breathe and "spit it out," the more my throat locked and tongue seized. He wasn't much of a help, but I think he probably knew that and didn't care. His way of fixing something was to impose his own will upon it. But my stuttering wasn't something he could fix; the more he tried the worse it got, and the worse it got the more frustrated he grew. Sensing that frustration, I clammed up around him and only spoke when spoken to.

School was no different. In fact, it was probably worse. There was nothing more frightening and humbling than standing in front of a classroom full of my peers, weak-kneed and short of breath, pulse thumping all the way to my toes, and not being able to put three words together without a freak show full of facial grimaces and oral gymnastics. I would have gladly allowed my eyes to be used for pincushions rather than to have to endure the torment of an oral book report or geography presentation.

But the most torment I received was at the hand of Marty Grubbs. Two grades ahead of me and fifty pounds heavier, Marty didn't know the meaning of the word mercy. Every morning during the fifth grade, he'd wait for me by my locker and pick through the lunch my mom had packed. More times than not he left me with only a lousy apple, and I'd go through the day with my stomach grumbling and my pride deflated.

Marty wasn't the brightest kid in Boomer Middle School but he was big for his age and had a mustache. Even the other seventh graders stayed out of his way. I knew I could outwit him but my tongue lagged so far behind my mind that I was no match, even for a lug like Marty Grubbs.

On the last day of fifth grade I went to school determined to stand my ground when Marty bared his fangs. He was waiting for me like always, arms crossed, leaning against my locker.

I stood before him, my arms hanging loosely at my sides like an Old West lawman itching to gun down the outlaw who'd wandered into town and stirred up trouble.

Marty held out his hand. "Give it here." I knew he meant my lunch.

"M-m-move, Mar-Marty."

But he didn't. He just stood there with his hand outstretched, palm up. "Give it here."

"N-no."

He pushed away from the locker and stood to his full height, pushed out his chest. "N-no?" Mockery was one of Marty's primary weapons. "Did you say n-no?" He poked my chest. "I said give it here, Snowflake."

"Not t-too-today. M-m-move."

"What, you think on the last day of school you can cheat me out of my lunch?"

My cheeks burned and I clenched my fists. There was so much I wanted to say to him, so much I had planned to say, but none of it would come out. My tongue froze behind my teeth and all I could get out was a guttural clucking sound.

"Tell me how you feel, Snowflake. C'mon, spit it out, you freak. Say it. Tell me." He moved his face closer and closer to mine until he was only inches away from my nose.

And that's when Annie stepped in and ruined the whole thing.

"Knock it off, Grubby," she said. "Leave him alone."

She reached out to shove him away but Marty was quick and caught her arm in his hand. He yanked and pulled her off balance. Annie lunged awkwardly and fell to the floor. I let out an indecipherable holler and swung my fist at Marty's face, hoping to hit anything. I missed. He sidestepped me, grabbed a handful of the back of my shirt and ran me into the lockers.

Sitting on my butt on the tile floor, my head spinning and face on fire, I noticed three things. One, all activity in the hallway had stopped. School fights have a way of doing that, of taking center stage with lots of spectators. Two, Annie had gotten back to her feet and had tears streaming down her cheeks. And three, Principal Spitzer was headed our way, hands behind his back, head cocked to one side.

All three of us spent the last day of school in Mr. Spitzer's office. Fortunately, Marty Grubbs moved to the neighboring town over the summer and he found a new school to terrorize.

***

The morning of Lizzy's first day of school, my mom made her a breakfast of French toast and scrambled eggs. Lizzy barely touched it. I could feel the tension emanating from her like heat from a light bulb. When it was time to leave, she didn't budge.

"Lizzy, it's time to go," I said, leaning over her chair.

But she didn't move and said nothing.

I knelt beside her. "Sweetie, we talked about this, remember? It's time to get back to school."

Tears welled in her eyes. "I'll miss you, Daddy."

"I know and I'll miss you, but we agreed that you'd do this. Remember?"

She nodded.

Part of me wondered if I was rushing things, if I should just give her the rest of the year off and she could do first grade over again next year. I wanted to be with her, to spend my time by her side. She was all I had left of our old life, of Annie. But part of me knew life went on and Annie would have wanted us to carry on and move forward. I pulled a photo of Annie from my shirt pocket. It was taken during one of our hikes just weeks before the accident. In the photo, she smiled earlobe to earlobe and dangled a garter snake from one hand. She was never afraid of that kind of stuff.

"Remember this?" I said, showing Lizzy the picture.

"That was when we went on our nature walk."

"Yeah. Remember Mommy picking up that snake and playing with it?"

Lizzy nodded. "It was gross."

"It sure was, but Mommy was brave, wasn't she?"

She studied the picture, her mother's face, the snake. "Yes."

I put the photo on her lap. "Keep that with you, okay? And be brave like Mommy. I know she's so proud of you right now. You've worked so hard in therapy and you've come so far." I kissed her head. "You'll do great. I know you will."

Boomer Elementary was nothing grand. As public schools go it was small, just one classroom per grade. The grounds were dotted with oak and sycamore trees, all beginning their fall conversion. Red and yellow leaves rustled along the cut grass, tossed about by a gentle breeze. I had lots of memories of the school, only a few of them good.

We walked through the front door, Lizzy using her walker, and immediately my chest tightened. I almost turned around and marched both of us out of there. Not much had changed. The floor was the same gray tile, the walls the same pale blue. And the smell of cleaning fluid, books, and children was just as I remembered it.

In the front office area, an elderly receptionist smiled and greeted us from behind a counter.

"Hi, this is Elizabeth Flurry, here for first grade." I'd called a week ago and made all the arrangements.

"Oh yes, we've been waiting for her." She stood and leaned over the counter so she could see Lizzy. "Hey, sweetheart, we'll get you settled into your classroom in just a minute."

After signing several forms, we met Principal Kittinger, who guided us on a quick tour of the school. The halls were decorated with brightly painted art projects and magazine-cutout collages. As I remembered, the cafeteria was in the same place, as were the library and bathrooms. I still could have found my way around that school with my eyes taped shut.

Finally, Principal Kittinger stopped outside a classroom and smiled. "Well, here you go. Welcome to the first-grade class of Mr. Grubbs."

I don't know if Kittinger noticed or not but my breath caught in my throat and I almost choked on it. Grubbs is not an unpopular name in the south. I knew that. But hearing it stirred up emotions and fears and anxieties I hadn't dealt with in twenty years.

"Let me get him." Kittinger stepped into the classroom and a minute later emerged with Lizzy's teacher.

It was him. Marty Grubbs. His face had changed, of course, matured, and his hair had a sprinkling of gray, but the mustache was the same. I tensed and a tingling started in the back of my head and shot all the way to my fingertips. I hadn't seen Marty since that last day of school, when we stepped out of the building and went our own ways. He shoved me and told me to watch my back, which I did for months until I realized he was just being Marty and his threat was toothless.

Kittinger put his hand on Lizzy's shoulder. "Mr. Grubbs, this is Elizabeth Flurry. She goes by Lizzy."

Marty bent at the waist and offered Lizzy his hand, which she timidly took. "Good morning, Lizzy. I'm excited to have you in our class." His voice hadn't changed much.

Kittinger motioned to me. "And this is her father, Ben."

Marty stuck his hand out and I hesitated before taking it. We were the same height now. I forced myself to look him in his eyes, hating the spiders still crawling up and down my arms.

There was a moment of awkwardness when the realization of who I was dawned in Marty's eyes. He looked away quickly and I knew then that he no longer had the advantage over me. That frightened little stuttering kid he used to bully was long gone.

I kissed Lizzy on the head and knelt before her. "You'll do fine, right?"

She nodded.

"Hey, I'll be here at three to pick you up. Do your best. You have your picture?"

She patted her sweater pocket.

"Okay, now go on. And have fun."

I watched through the door window as Marty led Lizzy, hobbling along in her walker, to the front of the class. I couldn't help but be afraid for my girl and wish there was another way. The other kids studied her like a pack of hungry wolves eyeing a lame rabbit, sizing her up, weighing her weaknesses. She was different and that would make her an easy target.

For the second time since Annie's death, I prayed. *God, protect her.*

CHAPTER 17

I PICKED LIZZY UP FROM school at exactly 3:15. Despite my deluge of questions, she didn't offer much information on the way home. She sat in the back seat of the truck, stared out the window, and gave me vague, one-word answers. I figured she was a bit shell-shocked and needed some time to decompress and process everything. Starting a new school was hard enough; starting a new school as a spectacle was doubly difficult. I'd give her some space then try again later on, maybe after dinner.

But as soon as we walked into my parents' home she burst into tears. The sobs came like waves of rain beating against her little body. Mom went for tissues while I led Lizzy to the sofa.

"Hey, now." I brushed her hair from her face. "What's the matter? What is it?"

She tried to speak but couldn't. Her words came out as coughed sobs.

Mom came back with the tissues and I handed one to Lizzy. "Shh, it's okay, baby. Just settle yourself first. It's okay now."

Lizzy hitched in a breath and blew it out, wiped at her eyes. I brushed more hair from her face. She wrung her hands as if she could get water from them. "They-they laughed at me."

"Who?"

"The other kids. Th-they said I walked like a retard."

Anger burned inside me like a stoked fire. Instantly I was transported back to fifth grade, standing in front of peers, stumbling and stuttering like an idiot while they snickered and sneered. The pain, the humiliation the fear, it was all there again. But this time my baby girl was absorbing those blows, my wounded and broken girl. I wanted the names of the kids, where they lived, their phone numbers. I wanted to find them and …

My mother's hand landed on my shoulder and squeezed. "Easy, Ben."

"Easy?" I pulled Lizzy to me and hugged her tight. "I'm not taking it easy." My voice quivered.

"Calm yourself." I'd heard her attempt to settle my dad with the same tone of voice.

Lizzy pulled away and reached into her sweater pocket. She pulled out the photo of Annie, sniffed, wiped fresh tears from her cheeks, and handed it to me. "And this happened."

The photo was wrinkled and scratched, smeared with dirt.

"How did this happen?"

Lizzy's mouth curved downward in a pitiful frown. Tears poured from her eyes. "I don't know. I-I was looking at it on the playground when-when a bunch of kids came up and started laughing at me. I-I dropped it."

"Did you tell Marty—Mr. Grubbs?"

She nodded.

I handed her another tissue. "And?"

"He didn't see it. He was playing dodgeball with some of the boys."

Stuffing the picture of Annie in my shirt pocket, I stood and kissed Lizzy on the top of her head. My watch said it was just after three-thirty. I thought teachers had to stay until four. If I left now I could catch Marty before he left for the day. We needed to have a chat.

"I'll be right back," I said, reaching for my keys.

My mom followed me to the door. "Where are you going?"

"The school. I need to talk to Marty."

***

When I arrived, Marty was in his classroom, at his desk. He looked up as I approached.

"Oh, hey, Ben, right?" He stood and offered his hand. I didn't take it. "Is something wrong?"

"My daughter, Lizzy, it was her first day today?" I couldn't hide the tension in my voice.

Marty glanced at his desk, moved the pen holder a quarter inch to the left, then stuck his hand in his pocket. "Yeah, listen—"

"She was pretty upset when we got home. You know why?"

"Look, Ben, if this is about what happened on the playground."

"It's about what happened all day. It's about this." I held up the picture of Annie and when I did some kind of anger that had been dormant in me for decades awakened. All I could see was the bully in front of me shoving my Annie to the floor. I hated him looking at her picture. It was something sacred, almost holy, a lasting remembrance of the only thing that was right in my life for so long. The photo shook in my hand.

Marty's shoulders slumped. "I'm sorry, Ben, really I am. I didn't see it happen. She told me about it and I did talk to the children involved."

"Is this the way it's going to be for her every day?"

"I don't know. Look, I'll talk to the kids again. But I can't be there every minute of the day, you know? Things happen. Kids do stuff. She had a tough first day. She cried some, kept mostly to herself. She's new ... different. You know how kids can be."

I put the photo back in my pocket. "Yeah, I know."

"Look, she's slower than the other kids, physically, and still emotionally dealing with a lot. Maybe she should be in the special needs class until things settle down."

All I heard was Marty Grubbs, the middle school bully, calling my daughter a freak. Before I had time to consider my reaction, my fist had formed and I swung at Marty's face, just like I'd done all those years ago. Only this time I hit my mark, right along the side of his nose, just under the eye. He grunted and spun around and stumbled back against the chalkboard. His hands groped for the chalk tray, but the blow had so disoriented him he missed and slumped to the floor.

Heart in my throat, my mouth suddenly dry, I spun around and stormed out of the room. In the hallway, I turned left and headed for the front door. A woman was there, another teacher. She looked at me and said, "Ben?" I only caught a glimpse of her face and it nearly stopped me but I had to keep moving, I had to get out of that building and catch my breath, find my head.

I got outside and found my car, bent at the waist, and almost vomited on the parking lot. My hand throbbed and my knees suddenly went very weak. I'd never hit anyone in my life and, with the exception of my one colossal whiff in fifth grade, had never even taken a swing at anyone.

I shut my eyes and saw her face, the teacher in the hall. I knew her. Amy Celio. I'd dated her in eleventh grade.

***

I fled to a place I hadn't visited in twelve years. It was remote, secluded, safe, and a storehouse of memories. Just a few miles from Boomer, the Cape Fear River twists and turns through the countryside like a sidewinder through tall grass. Overlooking one of those bends is Deadman's Rock, a granite outcropping that overhangs the river by no less than sixty feet. It's a popular place for couples to picnic and teenage boys to initiate themselves into manhood by Peter Panning off the ledge into the slow-moving river below. Over the years, more than one diver never climbed out of the water.

I parked my truck thirty feet below the rock and negotiated the dirt and gravel path that wound upward to its peak. When I'd reached the summit I tentatively walked to the edge and peered at the water below. It was dark and murky, just as I remembered it. Annie and I used to go here often just to sit and talk and get away from the turmoil that awaited us at home. It was our refuge, the place where we regained our sanity and got a better perspective on the world in which we lived. Up here, no one could bother us. There was no yelling, no screaming, no verbal assaults of any kind. Just the rocks and trees and whispering water below. The air was crisp and clean and imbued with the scent of dirt, leaves, and bark. Not even a hint of alcohol or tobacco. Trees crowded the far bank and spread out a forest for as far as the eye could see. This time of year the leaves were ablaze with a hundred shades of reds and oranges and yellows.

There at the ledge I sat on my butt and pulled my knees to my chest. The throbbing in my hand had settled some but the knuckles were still raw and tender. I couldn't believe I hit Marty. It was a good blow too. He'd remember it for a long time. But more than that I couldn't believe I'd seen Amy. I always liked her, just not as much as she liked me. We went on a few dates, had a good time together too. She had a quirky personality that drew me to her, put me at ease. But whenever I was with her I thought of Annie. I always thought of Annie. There was only room in my heart for one girl and it had always been her.

I heard footsteps behind me, shuffling on the dirt trail. I turned and watched until Becky came into view. She was breathing hard and put her hands on her knees.

"Boy, you sure picked a good place to hide," she said, wiping sweat from her brow.

I turned back around and picked up a stone, turned it over in my hand. "I'm not hiding. Just needed a place to think."

She sat next to me and crossed her legs. She smelled of sweat and perfume.

"How'd you find me?"

"Your mother called and said you'd stormed out of the house and were headed for the school. She was afraid you'd do something stupid."

I tossed the stone over the ledge and waited for the splash below, then picked up another one. "Did you go to the school?"

"Yep. And you did something stupid."

"How's Marty's face?"

"It'll heal."

I sent the stone sailing through the air. "Is he going to press charges?"

"I don't think so. I think he knows he had it coming."

"Maybe, but I shouldn't have done it."

She hesitated then sighed deeply. "Yeah, hitting people never solved anything. Why'd you do it?"

I shrugged. "I don't really know. It kind of just happened. For a second I saw the bully there again, but this time he was bullying my daughter."

"He's not like that anymore, you know."

"You think?"

She picked up a stone about the size of a golf ball, rolled it around in her hand, then tossed it over the edge. A second later it hit the water.

"People change, Ben. Boys grow up and become men. At least most do. Some never get the hang of the whole growing-up thing."

"He bullied me bad when we were kids." I didn't want to accept the fact that Marty could have changed, not the Marty Grubbs I'd known.

"I know he did. I was the only one Annie ever talked to about that stuff. Besides you."

A silent minute passed while both of us watched a pair of vultures ride a thermal high above the highest treetop. Finally, I said, "Why'd you come back here?"

She looked at her hands then back at the vultures. "To get away from California."

"What's so bad about California?"

"Brian."

"Your boyfriend?"

She turned her face to me. "*Ex*-boyfriend."

"What happened?"

Becky picked up another stone, cocked her arm, and gave it a toss. "Brian had a temper I didn't know about."

I didn't want to ask the question but felt I needed to. "Did he hit you?"

She smiled but it wasn't genuine. "He used to apologize after every time, beg me to forgive him, said how much he loved me and didn't want to hurt me and that he knew he needed help."

"But he never got that help."

"Nope. Every time I'd forgive him but every time my trust in him eroded a little more. It took a couple months of that for me to realize he wasn't ever going to get that help he knew he needed. I'm a slow learner. And I guess a glutton for punishment."

"So why did you come back here to live with your parents?"

Again, she put on that phony smile to hide the pain. "Brian didn't have a job so while we were living together we lived off my meager income as a barista in a local coffee shop. He liked to spend money. Loved the gadgets. So when I left I had next to nothing in my pockets, just enough to fly home."

"You didn't mind coming back home to your father?"

"Of course I minded. But where else was I supposed to go? I needed a place to stay while I got my feet back under me."

"How's he treating you?"

She shrugged. "Fine. He mostly stays out of my way. Stays out of everyone's way. He's turned all his anger inward. All he does is go to work, come home, sit in front of the TV."

"He's imploded."

"Exactly."

"Must be some life for your mom."

Becky bit her lower lip and hooked a few loose strands of hair behind her ear. "She'd rather have a zombie for a husband than Mike Tyson."

She stood and walked to the edge of Deadman's Rock and for a moment I thought she was going to do that Peter Pan thing into the Cape Fear River below. Her back to me, feet at the very edge of the precipice, she said, "You ever feel like there's parts of your past you just can't outrun? No matter how far or fast you go they keep catching up to you and reminding you how vulnerable you are?"

We'd come full circle back to Marty Grubbs. "Sure. And then you punch one of them in the face."

She turned her head a half turn giving me her profile. From that angle she looked even more like Annie. "You think I should punch my dad in the face?"

"Hitting people never solved anything," I said. "You said so yourself."

"Darn."

She was quiet a moment while she stood there, reminding me of that scene in *The Last of the Mohicans* where Alice inches to the edge of the cliff, looks at Uncas' dead body below, then at Magua, her captor, then drops off, finding the only freedom she could imagine.

Finally, Becky said, "Annie was always better at handling our home situation. She was the stronger one."

"She was always the stronger one. She was my rock."

"I didn't talk to her after I left for California. I regret that now."

I stood and stepped up next to her, my shoulder against hers. I'd always been afraid of heights but for some reason standing next to Becky brought some comfort. "We all have lots of regrets." In my mind I saw that intersection, the flash of lights, the semi's grill like a mouth full of metal teeth.

"Do we ever get rid of them?" She put her hand in mine. There was nothing romantic about the gesture. We shared a seat on the train of despair, the two of us; we'd both lost someone we loved dearly, someone who made our lives whole without us even realizing it.

"They tell me time heals everything," I said. "But I'm not sold on the concept."

Becky let go of my hand and wiped a tear from her eye. "I gotta go. Don't worry about Marty. He's not going to do anything." She turned and walked away and left me standing on the edge of the world by myself. Alone again.

CHAPTER 18

MOM WAS IN THE kitchen when I got home. The house smelled like spaghetti sauce and garlic bread, one of Lizzy's favorite meals. She glanced at me when I rounded the corner and sat on a barstool at the bar.

"I thought I was going to have to pick you up at the jail," she said, stirring the sauce with a wooden spoon.

"Would you have?"

She shrugged. "Eventually. In the morning."

"You would have left me there overnight?"

"Would you have deserved it?"

She had a point. If someone would have done that for my dad or Annie's dad a long time ago, things might have turned out much different for both our families. "Probably."

She put the spoon to her lips and tested the sauce. "What are you going to do?"

I'd made my mind up on Deadman's Rock. Somehow, being up there on top of the world like that with no distractions, no static, no busyness of the world around you, my thoughts were clear and decisions came easy. But now things were fogging up again. At some point during the drive home, the seed of uncertainty had wormed its way back in.

"I can't send her back there. She was traumatized."

"So what will she do instead?"

I picked up a fork that was sitting on the counter and touched each of the prongs with the tip of my finger. "I don't know yet. Maybe she just wasn't ready to go back. Maybe I forced her into it too early."

Mom stopped stirring the sauce long enough to look at me. "Don't do that to yourself, Ben. You didn't know what would happen."

"Didn't I?" I knew her limp and that cursed walker would make her an easy target. I knew from past experience that in school *different* wasn't the way to go. And I still sent her.

"You didn't know *that* would happen."

"Where is she?"

She motioned to the basement door. "With your father. She likes spending time with him. Have you noticed?"

Of course I'd noticed. I wasn't comfortable with it. No matter how many times my mom insisted he was a changed man, no matter what Lizzy thought of him. And I was afraid he'd prove me right and Lizzy would wind up getting hurt more than harsh words could ever do. I didn't answer my mother. Instead I set the fork down and headed for the basement.

At the bottom of the steps I stopped before rounding the corner and listened. Even though my dad couldn't put two coherent words together and make any kind of sense I listened to the tone of his voice. If I heard even the slightest hint of irritation or anger, that would be it. Lizzy would not be spending any more time with her grandpa.

"Do people ever laugh at you?" Lizzy's voice was somber and honest.

I didn't hear an answer but didn't see how anyone could laugh at my father. He never left the basement.

"Grammy said my daddy used to get teased because he stuttered." I'd never told Lizzy about my speech impediment and the ridicule it brought me. I never thought she needed to know that.

I peeked around the corner and saw Lizzy sitting beside the recliner, holding my dad's hand in both of hers. The TV was tuned to a news channel but the sound had been turned down.

"She said he used to come home crying and he would say he never wanted to go back to school."

My dad raised his free hand and rubbed his face then pointed a finger in the air. "He ... um, b-blue, went ... no ... g-good Monday, no." He waved his hand dismissively and shook his head.

Lizzy waited patiently but it was useless. Whatever he was trying to say was trapped in his head. Finally, she said, "It's okay. You don't have to talk if you don't want to. I like the way you listen."

My dad shook his head and pointed to his chest. "No, I ..." He stopped and drew in a deep breath. "I t-t-tell ... father ... bad-ly. No. Ahh." Again he shook his head and looked away.

"Is there something you need to tell my dad?"

"No. Y-yes. Yes." He nodded.

"Do you want me to get him?"

He seemed to think about that and, even after all these years, the idea of my dad actually wanting to talk to me, to hold a real conversation with me, made my pulse thump in my throat. "No."

"Can you write it down?"

"No."

"You should tell him sometime. It's not good to keep things inside."

She sounded so much like Annie. I pictured the two of them sitting on Lizzy's bed, legs crossed Indian-style, having a heart-to-heart about the need to speak honestly with each other and speak up if something is bothering you. Annie was good at those talks and I was glad she started imparting her wisdom to Lizzy at such an early age.

Dad nodded. "Yes. He ...um, h-he ... wants m-me ... um, singing ... No. No." And that was it. He was done.

Lizzy patted his hand. "It's okay. You'll get it out sooner or later. I know you will."

I ducked back behind the corner and went upstairs where my mom was still stirring the spaghetti sauce. Beside it, a pot of water boiled high. She dumped a handful of noodles into the water and stirred it with a wooden spoon.

I took my seat on the barstool again. "Mom, did Dad stutter as a kid."

"'Course he did. I thought you knew that."

"No, I didn't. He never told me."

"Where do you think you got it from?"

"I didn't know. I thought it was just one of those things."

She stopped stirring the noodles and went back to the sauce. "He stuttered bad all the way through school until he quit and went to work at the warehouse. Even there it was bad. When we met he could barely talk. He eventually just outgrew it though. Right after you were born. It was as

129

if having a son gave some purpose to his life and gave him the confidence he needed. 'Course, that's when all the anger started coming out too."

"Did he get teased?"

She paused and looked at nothing in particular on the countertop. "He used to talk about it sometimes, after he had a few beers in him. Yes, he was teased. He told me one time he got a new coat for Christmas. He was so proud to wear it to school because it was what was in fashion at the time. On the way home a group of boys followed him, making fun of his speech problem, mocking him, imitating him, you know."

Yeah, I knew all too well.

"When he got home he took his coat off and saw that the back of it was covered with mud. They were throwing mud at him." She stirred the noodles some more. "The teacher used to have him stand in front of the class and read his homework aloud, said it would help him overcome his fear of talking. Sometimes it would take him the whole class to get through one page."

She stopped stirring and reached across the counter to put her hand on mine. "Ben, there's a lot to your father that you don't know. He's had such a hard life."

"So why did he make things so hard for the rest of us too? He could have learned from that. He knew how potent words could be, how much they could hurt."

"Anger was all he knew."

I pulled my hand away and stood. "That's not good enough. Anger was all I knew too and I didn't go down that path with my family."

CHAPTER 19

MORNING CAME AFTER A restless and mostly sleepless night. At six thirty I got dressed, tiptoed downstairs, and found my mom in the kitchen, on her knees washing the floor.

"Don't you ever sleep?" I asked, pulling a ball cap on my head.

"'Course I sleep. But morning is the best part of the day. The house is quiet and I can get a lot done." She stood, straightening her knees slowly. "Want some breakfast?"

"No. I'm going to head over to Rosie's. I need some time to think about things, get my head about me."

"What do you want me to do with Lizzy?"

I glanced toward the steps. She was still sleeping soundly when I left the room. "Let her sleep. I'm going to keep her home from school until I decide what I'm going to do."

She hugged me and rubbed my back. There's something about a mother's hug that just feels right and this time it was no different. For a brief moment I had the feeling that everything would be okay. I wanted to stay in her arms a little longer, but she released me and put a hand on my cheek, a very motherly gesture. "I'm praying for you, Ben, and so is your father."

The thought of my dad praying was as foreign to me as hiking the Himalayas. My father and prayer were two things that didn't seem to fit in the same sentence. "I'll be back in a few hours," I said.

"Take your time. I'll make Lizzy a good breakfast."

I smiled. "I don't doubt that for a second. Thanks, Mom."

"And say hi to Rosie for me if you see her, okay?"

"Sure."

There are three food joints in Boomer: McDonald's, Waffle House, and Rosie's Good Eats. Rosie's had always been my favorite, not only because of the food but because of Rosie. When you were in her restaurant you were a member of her family. Rosie made it her business to know most of the folks in Boomer and what was currently happening in their lives. She knew who was having marriage issues, children issues, work issues, and church issues. But she wasn't a gossip or busybody. She knew because she genuinely cared, and that's what set her apart.

I pushed through the door to the jingle of an overhead bell and found a booth in the corner. The smell of bacon and coffee permeated everything. The place was busy but not full. In an hour it would be packed.

Moments later a middle-aged waitress I hadn't seen before approached and stood beside the table, tablet in hand. Her nameplate read "Nancy." "Mornin'. This your first time at Rosie's?"

"No. I used to live here in Boomer and come here all the time. I've been away for a while, though."

Her eyes brightened and mouth widened into a genuine smile. "Well welcome back."

"It's good to be back."

"What can I get ya, hun?"

It was as if I'd never left, as if I hadn't gone a full decade without sitting in one of these booths. And I knew exactly what I wanted without even looking at a menu. "Do you still have the breakfast specials?"

"Sure do."

"Great. Number five, please, with hot tea and a glass of water."

She wrote my order on her tablet and slid it into her apron. "It'll be ready in a jiffy."

The number five breakfast special was a farmer's omelet stuffed with green and red peppers, tomatoes, potatoes, onions, and cheese; griddle cakes; and a heaping pile of grits. I hadn't had a breakfast like that in years, not because Annie didn't make breakfast but because my job at the DEP required me to be on the road early, before my appetite kicked in.

Not long after Nancy disappeared into the kitchen area, the doors swung open and Rosie appeared, looked around, and found me. To know Rosie McCurdy is to experience her. Pushing no more than five feet and about as round as she is tall, her joy in what she does and easy friendliness is contagious. She has a thick southern drawl right out of *Gone with the Wind*, waddles when she walks, and snorts when she really gets laughing. But she has a way of making you feel welcome and wanted, of making you feel like your life is just as important to her as it is to you.

Rosie waddled over to my table, beaming like the morning sun, and motioned for me to stand up. "Well, ain't this a beautiful mornin'. Ben Flurry, stand up and let me see you."

I stood and she wrapped her arms around me. Reaching up, she cupped my face in her hands. "Look at you. My, aren't you a handsome thing. Sweetie, I'm so sorry for your loss. Annie was an angel, a bona fide angel."

"Yes, she was." I sat back in the booth and she took my hand.

"How are you and the little one doin'?" She kept her voice low, aware that our conversation was no one else's business.

"We're hanging in there, you know, good days and bad days." I almost told her about Lizzy's first day back at school but decided against it. She didn't need to know everything, at least not at once.

She squeezed my hand with both of hers. "Well, you keep on hangin' in there. I been prayin' for you. Lots of folk around here have."

"I appreciate that. Thanks. Mom says hi."

"Oh, how is your momma? I haven't seen her in ages."

"She's good. She's been a huge help."

"And how's your daddy?"

I wanted to say that he was getting exactly what he had coming to him but didn't. Instead I said, "He's okay. Mom says she hasn't seen much change in his condition in the past year or so."

She let go of my hand and looked at nothing in particular on the tabletop. "Poor man. Must be awful. Havin' so much to say and not bein' able to say any of it."

I knew Rosie wasn't ignorant to the man my father used to be. Everyone in Boomer knew he was a drunk with a big mouth. Apparently, she'd heard about his conversion and chose to forget his past sins. For a moment I wished I could be so forgiving. But the past wasn't so easy to let go of for me.

When I didn't respond she squeezed my shoulder and winked. "Don't worry about the tab on your breakfast, sweetie. This one's on the house."

I didn't want to take her charity but knew arguing with Rosie was as useless as trying to arm-tackle a charging bull. "Thanks, Rosie. That's nice of you."

She winked again and walked away. Minutes later Nancy returned with my food and I was knuckle-high in a farmer's omelet.

About halfway through my meal, a familiar voice interrupted me.

"Ben?"

I looked up and found Amy Celio standing there, coffee in one hand, brown bag in the other. She was tall and slender; the past twelve years seemed to have had no effect on her. She still looked every bit the eighteen-year-old she was the last time I saw her. Her hair was shorter now, bobbed at her shoulders, and held back with a wooden headband. She had always been a pretty girl and time had managed to enhance that quality.

She smiled. "Hey."

"Hey, Amy." A moment of awkwardness passed between us. The last time she'd seen me I was hurrying out of the school after punching Marty Grubbs in the face.

"So, I saw you yesterday," she said. "At the school."

I put my fork down and wiped my mouth with the napkin. My cheeks burned. "Yeah, about that—"

She held up the hand gripping the paper bag. "No need to explain. Marty told me what it was all about."

"Yeah. Pretty embarrassing." I motioned to the other bench. "You want to sit down?"

She looked at her watch. "Well, just for a minute. I have to get to the school. Just stopped here for my morning coffee and biscuits."

She sat and put her coffee and the paper bag on the table. Leaning in, she said, "Ben, I was so sorry to hear about Annie. How terrible. I was going to call you or send a card or something but I just didn't know what to say."

"It's okay. You don't need to apologize."

"Are you and your daughter doing all right?"

"We're getting along. Obviously things didn't go so well introducing Lizzy to school."

She dropped her eyes to her hands and I followed them, noticing she wore no rings. "Sorry about that. Kids can be so mean. I was sick when Marty told me."

"What grade do you teach?"

"Second."

"So you'll have Lizzy next year." I didn't miss the glimmer of hope that flashed in her eyes.

"So you're planning on staying in Boomer?"

I shrugged. "I'm not sure yet. I need to get my feet under me again. Get a grip on things first, then we'll see how the future looks."

Amy checked her watch again. "I have to go." She reached across the table and put her hand over mine, held my eyes in a steady gaze. "Ben, if you ever need someone to talk to, just to listen, I'm here, okay?"

Then, as if she realized the uncomfortableness of the moment, she pulled her hand away and stood abruptly. "I'll see you around?"

"Probably here and there."

And then she was gone and I was left rubbing my hand. Her touch had stirred something inside me. Something I wasn't sure I was comfortable with.

***

Evening arrived early after a thick cloud cover moved into the Cape Fear River valley, and with it the temperatures had taken a dip. After dinner I left Lizzy and Mom to clean up and headed for the front porch with a cup of tea and my sweatshirt. There's something about a porch and a rocking chair that draws Southerners to it. Maybe it's the fresh air or the cooler evening temperatures, or maybe just that there never seems to be anything better to do. Life moves along at an easy pace in the South and not too many people are in a hurry to do anything. Living up north in Pennsylvania I'd forgotten what it felt like to pass the time doing nothing. Now that I'd had a few days to adjust my speed and slow everything down, I liked it.

I listened to the familiar creak the rocker made as it moved back and forth on the porch boards. The crickets were warming up for the night and daylight was waning quickly, deepening the colors of the leaves that had yet to fall. Inside, I heard the clatter of pots and plates and silverware and the muted conversation of my mother and daughter.

Thanksgiving was in a week and I'd decided earlier to keep Lizzy home from school until after the holiday then we'd try it again, but not until I'd had a sit-down discussion with both the principal and Marty. I didn't want a repeat of what had already happened.

My parents' home sat back down a gravel lane about a quarter-mile from the paved road. There were only two homes along the lane, theirs and the Flemings'. From beyond the trees I heard the crunch and pop of tires on stones. As the sound grew louder, I glanced over at the Flemings' driveway. Becky's car was there as was her parents' SUV. The approaching vehicle, a green 1990s Ford pickup, finally came into view and pulled into our driveway. The engine shut off. With so little light left, I couldn't see the driver parked under the shade of the trees. The door opened and a man stepped out, smoothed his jacket, and closed the door. It was Marty Grubbs.

Marty walked up to the porch steps, hands in his pockets, and kicked at some gravel. At first I wasn't sure if he'd come for revenge or just to chew me out, maybe tell me he had indeed pressed charges and I'd soon be hearing from his attorney. But when he looked up I saw no malice in his face at all. In fact, he appeared downright humble, a foreign concept to the Marty Grubbs I used to know. His left eye was puffy around the cheekbone and bruised all the way to the ear. It looked sore and I couldn't help but feel bad, despite the satisfaction such a sight brought.

"Hey, Ben," he said.

I nodded. "Hey."

"Mind if we talk a spell?"

I pointed at the other rocking chair. "Got an empty chair and lots of time."

He climbed the three steps and sat in the rocker, crossed his legs and laced his fingers together.

"How's your eye?" I said.

He touched his cheekbone. "Tender, but it'll be all right."

"Sorry about that. I don't know what got into me."

He waved off my apology. "I deserved it. It was actually about twenty years too late. Look, Ben, I'm real sorry about Lizzy. It shouldn't have happened. And while I'm at it, I know it doesn't mean anything now but I'm real sorry for how I treated you when we were kids. I was pretty screwed up then, lots of stuff going on at home, but it's all excuses now."

I accepted his apology. No matter what I thought of the seventh-grade version of Marty Grubbs, it took a big man to apologize for past sins, especially after being socked in the face. "Thanks. Do you know where she's coming from?"

"You mean what happened?"

"Yeah."

He looked at his hands and twisted his fingers. "Becky told me. You two have been to hell and back."

"At times it feels like we're still there," I said. "What's important now, though, is Lizzy."

"Will she ever come back to school?"

"I think we'll try again after the Thanksgiving holiday. How's that sound?"

Marty nodded. "Whatever you and her decide. And I'll make sure she's treated right."

"Just treated like everyone else will do."

"You got it."

I took a sip of tea. "Would you like something to drink?"

He smiled. In the South, inviting someone onto your porch and offering them a drink is like a handshake and a hug. I was telling him the past was officially in the past and he knew it. "No thanks. I best be getting along. Gotta get ready for tomorrow."

We shook hands and I watched as he got into his truck and pulled away. And I was left wondering why I had such an easy time forgiving Marty, but wouldn't think of extending the same mercy to my father.

CHAPTER 20

THE SUNDAY BEFORE THANKSGIVING, Lizzy wanted to visit Annie's gravesite. Whether it should have or not, her request didn't catch me by surprise. I knew she'd want to go there sooner or later. I'd told Lizzy earlier that Annie wasn't really there, that her mommy was in heaven with Jesus. She asked me why Jesus wanted her with him instead of letting her live with us. I didn't have an answer. I didn't know what spurred her desire to visit the site but I guessed it was because the Saturday before Thanksgiving reminded her of Annie and of our family tradition. On that day every year we trekked into the Pennsylvania hinterland and cut down a fresh Christmas tree. Actually, it was a tree farm, but it was remote and we pretended to be settlers celebrating our first Christmas on the homestead.

The cemetery was situated on a square of acreage located outside the town of Boomer. The oldest tombstones dated back to the 1780s. The terrain was hilly and uneven, not conducive to a walker or wheelchair, so I enlisted Becky to help get Lizzy to Annie's site. Me on her right, Becky on her left, we held hands and took our time.

Annie's plot lay about a hundred yards off the beaten path, in a corner of the cemetery populated by centuries-old live oaks grizzled with beards of silvery-gray Spanish moss. On a warm summer evening, the corner would have been alive with the aroma of the moss's tiny blooms, but this time of year it smelled of decaying leaves and moist soil. We arrived at the place where Annie lay and all stood silently before her marker. It was made of polished gray granite and said only what needed to be said. Annie's name, birth date, death date, "Wife. Mommy. Friend." I squeezed Lizzy's hand and knew Becky was doing the same thing.

In my right hand I carried a bouquet of assorted flowers and handed it to Lizzy. Still holding my hand, she bent at the waist and positioned the flowers next to the stone with great care. When she stood again she said, "Mommy would like those flowers."

"Yep. She would," I said. "She loved flowers, didn't she?"

Lizzy looked up at me and I saw the tears in her eyes. "Do you think Mommy likes flowers in heaven?"

"You betcha." Tears pushed their way to my eyes now too. "And I bet she's surrounded by them in heaven. The most beautiful flowers you've ever seen."

A slight smile curled the corners of Lizzy's mouth. She liked the idea of that. "They probably smell really strong there. She liked to smell flowers."

Annie was one of those people who took time to smell the roses, any flowers for that matter. "They probably have flowers there that we don't even have here on earth."

Lizzy's eyes widened. "Oh, she's gotta love that. New flowers to smell and look at."

We were all quiet for a few moments, paying our respects, remembering, grieving. Finally, Lizzy turned her face toward me and said, "Daddy, how do we know Mommy's in heaven? I mean, how do we really know?"

I thought for a moment. "Well, she was a Christian, right?"

"Yes. She told me how to be a Christian."

"She sure did. She had Jesus in her heart. He was her Savior."

"Just like me. And you."

"That's right. And the Bible says that if we have Jesus as our Savior, then when we die we'll go to be with him and he's in heaven. It's his promise."

"And he never breaks a promise, right?"

"Right." But even as I agreed with my daughter's declaration I had my own questions about its veracity. Wasn't there some kind of promise about ripping wives from husbands, mothers from children? Wasn't there a promise of protection from hurt and abandonment, from pain that tore at the soul and made one question his will to go on living? What good were all the other promises if suffering was so close, so real, so right now?

Satisfied, Lizzy turned to Becky. "Aunt Becky, do you believe in Jesus?"

"Uh, well," Becky smiled and pushed a strand of hair behind her ear. "Sure. Sure I do." She glanced at me, then away, but I didn't miss the shadow of doubt in her eyes.

"I can't wait to see Mommy again."

I swallowed past the lump forming in my throat. *Please God, don't let it be sooner than it needs to be.*

Suddenly, Lizzy straightened up and said, "I'm ready to go now, Daddy."

But I wasn't ready yet. "Why don't you two head back to the car awhile and I'll catch up."

"Hey, little girl," Becky said, "you want a piggyback ride to the car?"

Lizzy's eyes widened and she smiled. "Yeah." She looked at me for approval.

"It's okay with me if your aunt doesn't mind."

Becky turned around and squatted. "Climb on, squirt. You can't be that heavy."

I helped Lizzy onto Becky's back and watched as they disappeared around a stand of black gum trees. Shoving my hands in my pockets, I turned back to the gravesite. For some reason beyond what I knew, I felt close to Annie here. I knew it was nothing more than a plot of dirt covering her remains but I felt close to her spirit or maybe her memory. Maybe it was just that seeing her name, her birthday, what she lived for, engraved in stone, sparked memories I'd not thought about, stirred emotions I'd not felt, dug up hurts I thought I was dealing with. Maybe it was just that she felt *emotionally* close.

On the drive over I'd told myself I wasn't going to talk to a stone. Annie wasn't really there and wasn't going to talk back. And whether she could even hear me from her place in heaven, I had no idea. I'd always thought people who talked to the dead were either desperate or deluded. But standing there on that ground, a light breeze rustling through the Spanish moss and what leaves were left on the oak, I must have felt desperate, because I started talking.

"I think about that night all the time, you know. The accident. I could have prevented it. I should have. I never told you—I never got a chance to—how sorry I am. Lizzy's doing better. She's still using a walker but I think she'll be able to give it up soon."

Tears pooled in my eyes and blurred my vision of Annie's stone. I did nothing to wipe them away. I wanted them to come; I needed to get it out.

"She looks so pitiful hobbling along with that thing. Every time I see her walking it feels like my heart gets ripped out all over again. And to know it was my fault, that I'm responsible for her suffering. I'll never forgive myself."

Before I finished saying it I could hear her voice in my head: *Benjamin Flurry, don't you blame yourself for this. It was no one's fault. It just happened.*

"I miss you, Annie. So does Lizzy. We're not supposed to live without you. That wasn't part of the deal. I'm scared. How am I supposed to raise a daughter on my own?"

I thought I felt Lizzy's hand on my hip and spun around, but no one was there, only the trees and moss and falling leaves.

Annie told me once soon after we were married that if anything ever happened to her she'd want me to remarry, to be happy and go on living. She said there'd be no need for both of us to die. But I couldn't imagine another woman taking her place, not now, not ever. There was always only room in my heart for one girl, Annie Fleming. And that's the way it would always be.

I bent forward and touched the stone. It was cold and solid and lifeless.

"I promised to love and to cherish you until death parted us but I can't give it up just because you're not here anymore. I'll always love you. It's in my DNA now. It's part of who I am."

I allowed my fingers to linger on the stone a little longer, then slid them off and headed back to the car, back to life without Annie. Back to the vacuum she'd left.

CHAPTER 21

G ROWING UP, THANKSGIVING AT our house was never a big deal. Both my mom's parents died at an early age and my dad's mother didn't want anything to do with him. For him, the feeling was mutual. I had one aunt on my mother's side, Aunt Clarice, and she lived a very contented life in Minneapolis with her husband and three boys. We never saw them. My father had three brothers who were usually just as drunk and ornery as he was. When they got together the fireworks started so Mom did her best to keep them separated.

That meant Thanksgiving at our house was pretty much just another day, except Mom would make cranberry sauce and stuffing to go with the turkey, mashed potatoes, and snaps. Dad had the whole day off, which didn't give Mom and me much to be thankful for. He sat around and watched football while he nursed his beer until dinner was ready, then he'd make up a heaping plate and return to his spot in front of the TV. Normally he'd fall asleep in that chair, pants unbuttoned, food on his shirt, an empty beer can by his side.

Annie's family was different in more than a few ways. Thanksgiving was a big deal in their house. Since both her parents' families were in Illinois and didn't want to make the trip to Boomer, the Flemings threw a Thanksgiving Day celebration for the whole church. They attended the only Catholic church in town and I think every member stopped by that house for the free food and town gossip.

Annie hated Thanksgiving Day at her house, she'd told me on more than one occasion. Her dad, a deacon at the church, didn't drink a drop all day, didn't even put the wine out. He was too pious for that. But when the crowd had dispersed and the food had been scraped from the plates, the beer started flowing. And after about an hour he was drunk enough to start swinging at Annie and Becky. That's when she would flee the home and hide away in my treehouse. There she'd wait until after midnight, when Mr. Fleming was good and asleep, drowned in his alcohol, then sneak back into the house. By morning he'd be so hungover he couldn't swing a baseball bat at a barn and hit it.

One Thanksgiving in particular stands out, though not because the day brought anything out of the ordinary (every Thanksgiving Day was the same), but because of what happened when the sun had set and the Fleming guests had gone home and Mr. Fleming had turned into Mr. Hyde.

I was on our front porch, sipping a Coke and rocking myself to sleep while Dad dozed in front of the TV and Mom washed the dishes. I heard the screen door of Annie's home creak open and slam shut, heard her father yell a string of obscenities, and saw Annie go darting across her yard to the oak tree in the corner of ours. Through the darkness I could just make out her form climbing the ladder to the treehouse.

Casually, I set down my soda can and left the porch, made my way to the back of the yard, and stood at the base of the tree.

"Annie?"

She didn't answer but I could hear her soft whimper above me.

"Annie, can I come up?"

Still no answer.

I carefully climbed the ladder and poked my head through the opening in the treehouse floor. She was in the corner, knees pulled to her chin. The sound of her soft crying twisted my heart. I knew what had happened; we'd been down this road too many times. I pulled myself into the house and crawled to where she was. "Did he hit you?"

She shook her head and wiped at her tears.

I sat next to her, close enough that our shoulders touched. I was fourteen and at the age where I noticed girls, their figures, their aroma, their touch. And being so close to Annie always stirred something inside me.

"What happened?"

She pulled the back of her hand across her eyes and sniffed twice. "He's such a hypocrite."

This was not new information. Both of our fathers went to church, sat in the pews, sang the songs, and drank coffee and socialized afterward. And both our fathers were drunks. The difference was that everyone knew my dad was a drunk; Annie's father had somehow managed to keep his vice a secret, which made him twice the hypocrite.

"You should have heard him in there today," she said. I could hear the contempt in her voice. "Talking like he was all holier than thou. Discussing theology stuff with Father Howe, can you believe it? Father Howe thinks the world of him, I know he does, but he has no idea what kind of man he is. He's got the world fooled."

"So what happened?"

"Nothing. I mean, he's in one of his moods. He hasn't hit anyone yet."

"I could hear him yelling."

Annie was quiet for a moment. She stared at the floor and let tears roll down her cheeks. When she spoke her voice was quiet and shaky. "He called me a whore."

"Why?" Not that it mattered. Nothing mattered with Mr. Fleming. Nothing made sense when he was drunk.

She shrugged. "Who knows. He thinks you and me ... you know."

Impulsively, I reached my arm around her shoulders and pulled her closer to me. "He doesn't know you."

She put her head on my shoulder and I knew then I wanted to marry Annie Fleming. I wanted to spend the rest of my life with her head on my shoulder. Though the outside world raged with violence and hypocrites and flowed with alcohol and lies, at that moment, life was perfect in that tree house. And I promised myself I'd fight to make sure it stayed that way.

CHAPTER 22

THE DAY BEFORE THANKSGIVING, my mom sent me to the Piggly Wiggly for a small dump truck load of groceries. She said it would be a Thanksgiving meal we'd never forget ... to honor Annie and celebrate Lizzy's and my homecoming. But it still didn't feel like a homecoming. In so many ways, I felt like a stranger.

I still hadn't found any work around Boomer. I'd put in an application with the local park service, the North Carolina Department of Environmental Protection, even a local private school looking for a science teacher, but so far hadn't gotten even a nibble. Times were tough for anyone seeking employment. My mom suggested working for the warehouse, said there were always opportunities there. I could work as a picker or loader or maybe even jump right in as a foreman. But something inside me, something deep down close to my soul rejected that idea like it was last week's meat that'd been left out too long and now smelled foul. For one, I didn't want to give my dad the pleasure of knowing that after I'd spent all that money on a big college education I still wound up pushing boxes at the warehouse. And two, I felt to take a job like that would be betraying the dream Annie and I had entertained since we were kids. The dream of getting out of Boomer, making something better for ourselves, being on our own and raising our own family. It was one thing to move back in with my parents on a temporary basis, but taking a job at the warehouse felt too permanent. Like I would be allowing fate, that scaly tentacle that had its grip on every boy and girl born in Boomer, North Carolina, to slap a blue collar on me and keep me here forever.

At the Piggly Wiggly, I grabbed one of the big carts, pulled the list Mom had given me from my pocket, and placed it on the child's seat in the cart. A memory flashed through my mind, just as quick as a race car whizzes by at one of the big tracks. Annie and me and Lizzy at the supermarket in Pennsylvania. Lizzy sitting in that seat, waving at the other shoppers, smiling ear to ear, laughing. Annie pulling items from the shelf, humming a tune and crossing off her list as she walked. She'd give me a small list, I'd retrieve what I could remember, then get my next set of orders and go for more. Every time I rounded an aisle, arms loaded down with boxes of cereal and jars of spaghetti sauce, and saw my wife and daughter, my heart took a skip and I'd pause and look at them, watch how they interacted with each other, with passing shoppers. Annie always had a smile on her face and that joy naturally rubbed off on Lizzy. It was at moments like that I'd feel such contentment it would almost bring me to tears.

Outside the main doors to the Piggly Wiggly, a lump lodged in my throat and I had to stop and compose myself before entering. That contentment was gone now, replaced with a hole the size of the largest crater on the dark side of the moon. Annie was my rock, the foundation on which my life had been built, and now I had nothing but shifting gravel beneath my feet.

Twenty minutes later I had most of the items on my list crammed into the cart. I was amazed at how well I remembered where things were. It had been at least eleven years since I last shopped there. I bought a six-pack of Cokes, right before leaving for Penn State, that morning I pledged my love to Annie. It seemed like such a long time ago now, like a whole lifetime had passed. I could have been eighty and a widower and it wouldn't have felt any different.

In the produce section, as I scanned the display for the asparagus, a woman behind me said, "Funny to run into you here, Ben Flurry."

I turned and found Amy Celio with an empty cart. She was wearing a pair of faded jeans and a fitted, long-sleeve shirt with some ruffles around the hem. It looked like something Annie would have worn.

"Oh, hey, Amy. Hi." I pointed at my stuffed cart. "Yeah, just getting some things for Thanksgiving tomorrow."

"Are you cooking?" She smiled as if she already knew the answer. Amy always had a nice smile. It was one of the things about her that first attracted me all those years ago.

"Uh, no. My cooking skills are very limited." I motioned toward her cart. "How 'bout you? You here to stock up?"

She shrugged. "Just getting a few things. A few years ago my parents up and moved to Idaho."

"Idaho?"

"Yeah, can you believe it? My dad always wanted to live in northern Idaho, so when he retired they sold their home here and went. They love it."

"Are you going there tomorrow?"

Amy looked at her hands. "No. It's too expensive to fly out there and what with the all the hassle and everything. I was out there over the summer for a few days. It's beautiful country."

Amy never had a close relationship with her parents. An only child, she was home alone much of the time as her parents either worked or spent their time socializing with anyone who mattered in Boomer and the surrounding area. She'd told me once years before that she thought her parents never intended to have children and saw her as a nuisance. She was practically raised by babysitters.

I knew from the way she spoke and her empty cart that Amy would be alone for Thanksgiving and I knew I should invite her to my parents' house. Part of me wanted to. After all, I'd dated Amy a few times when I was seventeen and she was sixteen. We had a good time together too. She was outgoing and pleasant, quick to laugh, and always easy on the eyes. But she had one mark against her: she wasn't Annie. I knew I broke her heart that day I told her we shouldn't see each other anymore. She was a smart girl and probably saw it coming. She knew why. But to her credit, she never spoke ill of me, didn't avoid me in the halls or try to compete for my attention. I think on some level she knew Annie and I were right for each other, that according to the Higher Power we were meant to be together.

But because of the history we shared there was a part of me that didn't want to invite her. Amy had only grown more attractive with age and maturity, and there was a vulnerability about her that stirred something inside me. But it was on a purely physical level, born of hormones and desire, and I didn't want to go there. The very thought of it spoke of betrayal and unfaithfulness. I wasn't ready to deal with that kind of guilt.

"Who will you be spending Thanksgiving with then?" I said.

She found her hands again and glanced at them. "No one. I'll probably spend the day getting caught up on work or maybe I'll go into school and work on Christmas decorations. The kids always love how I decorate the room."

I felt pity for Amy. In some weird way, though I was surrounded by those who loved me—Lizzy, my mom, Tom back in Pennsylvania—I knew the kind of loneliness she battled. It was the kind that was held at bay as long as you stayed active, kept your mind occupied and hands busy. But at night, when the house was quiet and lights were down, it crept in and sat in your head like a lump of granite, cold and hard and unmoving.

Before I could stop myself, the words came out, as if my lips had decided to secede from the rest of my body and do their own thing. "You could come over my parents' for dinner tomorrow. If you're not doing anything else, of course."

Amy shook her head. "Oh, I couldn't intrude like that. I mean, it's your first Thanksgiving since ..." She dropped her eyes and her cheeks flushed red as her words trailed off.

She didn't have to finish. It was our first Thanksgiving without Annie and she didn't want to be the awkward replacement.

It was too late to backpedal. "Oh, no, please," I said. "It's okay. It's no intrusion at all."

"Do you think your mother would mind?"

"No. Of course not." I looked at the cart, nearly overflowing with food. "We have enough here to feed half of Boomer."

"Great. That's so nice of you to invite me. Are you sure there's enough and your mom won't mind?"

"Positive."

"What time?"

Great question. I had no idea. "Well, we used to always eat at five. Why don't you come by then and if it's earlier than that I'll call you and let you know."

She gave me her cell number and said, "Or if anything else comes up, feel free to call."

I knew what she meant, that if I ever just felt like talking, she was a willing and good listener. "Okay. Thanks." I pocketed my phone. "Well, I guess I better get going. See you tomorrow."

She put her hand on mine like she had in the diner. Her touch was soft and again stirred that something inside me. "Thanks, Ben. You don't know how much it means to not have to spend Thanksgiving alone."

"You're welcome. We'll see you around five."

"Great."

As I walked away, a different kind of guilt squirmed in my chest. I didn't want to lead her on. Amy was a smart and sensitive woman, I remembered that about her, and she had to know it was too soon for anything to develop between us, but she had battled the loneliness demon a lot longer than I had. I needed to be careful. I wasn't ready for any kind of relationship and certainly wasn't ready to love again. Not yet and probably not ever.

***

When I came home from the store there was a vehicle parked in front of my parents' home. There were a lot of maroon Chevy Blazers out there but there was only with a Pennsylvania plate that would be sitting in my parents' gravel driveway. Tom had come to visit. I felt a very heavy weight lift from my shoulders, as if someone had reached down and snatched it away, and tears slipped into my eyes. I needed to see my old friend. I needed to talk to him. Though I hadn't met him until after Annie had gone, he was my only link to our life in Pennsylvania, the life I'd shared with Annie. He was a portal for memories I would otherwise have no means of accessing.

Shutting off the truck, I scooped up two bags of frozen and refrigerated items and headed for the house. I wanted to drop the bags and wrap Tom in a bear hug, but when I pushed through the front door he wasn't there, greeting me with that wide, white smile. Mom was in the kitchen, humming a tune and Lizzy was at the counter, perched on a barstool, scooping the good stuff out of a pumpkin.

Lizzy spun around on the stool when she heard me coming and nearly fell off. "Daddy, guess who's here?"

I put the bags on the counter and kissed my daughter on the forehead. "I saw his Blazer out there. Where is he?"

"He's in the basement with your father," Mom said. "Those two hit it off as soon as they met."

A twinge of irritation dampened my cheery mood. Tom was my friend and I didn't want my dad getting his attention. Fact was, Tom was more of a father figure to me than my dad ever had been.

"When did he get here?" I asked.

"Right after you left," Lizzy said. "You just missed him."

Mom ran her hands under a stream of water then dried them. "I invited him," she said. "I hope you don't mind."

"Mind? No way. It'll be great to see him again." I'd spoken to Tom several times on the phone since moving back to North Carolina but this would be the first time I saw him since we pulled away from our house in Pennsylvania, leaving him on the front porch, waving and grinning. Lizzy had cried for the first hour of the trip and I did my best not to join her.

"You should go on down and let him know you're here," Mom said. "He said he'd help you carry in the groceries when you got home."

I descended the basement stairs and stopped in the same place I'd stood to listen to Lizzy and my dad talk. There I could remain out of direct sight and still hear what was being said. Tom's distinct, low voice resonated in the basement.

"I think deep down he knows, Mistuh Flurry. He just don't want to admit it yet. Give him time. He'll come 'round."

I knew he was talking about me. Already, my dad had pulled Tom onto his side and positioned me as the hard-hearted prodigal son who had returned home with a chip on his shoulder and was unwilling to just forgive and forget a lifetime of wrongs and abuse.

Poking my head around the corner, being careful not to be seen by Tom, I watched as my friend took my dad's hand in both of his. Tom leaned in close. His eyes were intense and the shadows that fell across his face made him look ten years older.

"You keep lovin' him," he said, his voice lower now, "and he'll come 'round. You watch. He'll see the diff'rence in you. It's a diff'rence only God can make so only God can open someone's eyes to it, really."

My dad had always been the biggest bigot I knew. Didn't matter the color of the skin, if it wasn't white there was something wrong with the person. They wore a target that he loved to take shots at. The old Walter Flurry would welcome a rabid bobcat into our house and offer it his first-born (me) before he tolerated a black man under his roof. And I heard him say before that he'd rather put his hand in molten lava than shake hands with a black man. And now here he was, not only talking to a black man but holding his hand. My eyes knew what they were seeing but my mind refused to accept it. It couldn't be that easy.

I tiptoed back up a few stairs then came down again, making sure to produce enough sound to alert them of my arrival. When I rounded the corner Tom was no longer holding my dad's hand. He stood and smiled that wide smile of his and opened his arms.

"Well, well," he said, taking steps toward me. "Now there's the man I came to see."

He wrapped me in a hug and nearly squeezed the breath out of me. Then, holding me at arm's length like a father would his child, he laughed and said, "How you been, my friend?"

I shrugged, glanced at my dad. "We're doing okay. Hanging in there."

"Sure was nice of your momma to invite me."

"I'm glad she did and glad you could make it."

"Are there still groceries in the car?"

"Bags full."

He slapped my shoulder. "Good." Then, turning, he put his hand on my dad's shoulder and said, "I'm gonna go help your son unload the car, Mistuh Flurry. It sure was good talkin' to you."

My dad smiled and nodded. He looked up at Tom and for the first time in my life I saw admiration in his eyes. "You, uh, boxed ... no. Uh, travel, come." Finally, he shook his head in frustration and waved his hand.

Tom patted his shoulder. "I'll be sure to come down a little later and we can finish our conversation."

Dad smiled again and put his hand over Tom's.

After dinner was gone and the plates cleaned, Tom disappeared back down to the basement and I stayed in the kitchen to help my mom dry and put the dishes away. Lizzy was on the sofa in the living room reading a book.

"Thanks for inviting Tom," I said, wiping water from a dinner plate. "It sure is nice to see him again."

"He's a wonderful man."

"He helped Lizzy and me so much after Annie's death. I don't think we would have made it without him."

Mom handed me another plate. "I'm glad you have a friend like him."

I wiped that plate down and placed it in the cupboard. "Mom, I ran into someone at the Piggly Wiggly and invited her for dinner tomorrow. I hope it's okay."

She stopped drying and looked at me with big eyes. "'Her'?"

"Amy Celio. You remember her?"

"Sure I do. She teaches at the elementary school now, doesn't she?"

"Yeah. Her parents moved to Idaho and she was going to spend Thanksgiving alone."

Mom took to drying a saucepan. "Well, that was nice of you to invite her."

"Is it okay? I mean, we'll have enough. I didn't know Tom was coming too and that man can put away some food."

Mom laughed. "We'll have plenty."

There was a moment of silence between us until finally my mom glanced into the living room at Lizzy on the sofa, legs stretched out, nose in her book, and said, "Are you sure you're ready for this?"

I knew what she was thinking. "It's not like that, Mom."

She put her hand on my arm. "I'm sorry. I shouldn't have assumed anything."

"I don't know if I'll ever be ready."

Mom squeezed my arm. "You and Annie had something special. You don't have to replace her."

Tears pushed behind my eyes and my chin quivered. I nodded, fearful that if I opened my mouth the dam would let loose and the tears would gush. I didn't want to do that in front of my mom, and not with Lizzy in the next room.

Later, after tucking Lizzy into bed and kissing her goodnight, I turned out the light in her room and blew her another kiss at the doorway.

"Dad," she said, pushing herself up on her elbows.

"Yeah, sweetie." I walked back over to her bed and sat on the edge of the mattress. "What is it?"

"I like having Mr. Tom here."

"So do I."

She paused while she bit her lower lip. "I don't know why, but when he's around I feel closer to Mommy."

I knew exactly how she felt. I ran my hand over her head then caressed her cheek. "Me too."

"Why is that? Mr. Tom never knew Mommy."

"Well, I think in a way he does know her from all the things we've told him about her."

She thought about that. "He makes me think of home too."

For Lizzy, home was the last place where we were a family. All of us together. Our house in Pennsylvania. "Yeah, I know. Seeing Tom again makes us think of our old house and when we think of the old house we think of Mommy, right?"

She smiled. "Exactly. Do you still think about her a lot?"

I ran my thumb over her eyebrow. "Every minute of every day. She's always with me."

"Me too. I pretend she's here and imagine what she'd say about certain things. If I try real hard I can almost hear her voice. Do you think I'll ever forget what she sounded like?"

Most likely she would. Over time the memory of Annie would fade and Lizzy's little brain would crowd out the sound of her mother's voice. I would have to do my best to make sure that didn't happen. "I'll tell you what," I said. "To make sure that doesn't happen, we'll watch some of those old videos we have. That way you'll keep hearing her voice and never forget it."

Again, the smile was there. I loved Lizzy's smile. "That's a great idea, Dad."

"Okay, now, I'm gonna sit on the porch for a little while. I'm just downstairs, so if you need anything just holler. All right?"

"Gotcha."

I kissed her again, first on the forehead then on the cheek. "Good-night, gooney bird."

She laughed. "Dad, Mommy used to call me that."

"When you'd do something silly."

"Yup."

"I don't want you to forget. I love you, darling."

"I love you too, Daddy."

***

Outside, the sky was dark and the air was cool and damp and smelled of ozone. In the distance, over the rooftop of the Fleming place, the sky lit up. Seconds later the deep growl of thunder rumbled through the clouds.

I sat in the rocker on the porch and tipped my head back, closed my eyes, and listened to the sound of nature gearing up for a real show. For some reason it reminded me of the time I almost lost Annie.

It was the summer of my thirteenth birthday and I was full of spit and confidence. Being a teenager was a big deal. Annie and I went down to the river to hunt crawfish. I told her I knew of a great little pool where there were so many you just reached your hand in and pulled them out like cookies from a jar.

By the time we got there the sky was gray as slate and textured like a freshly plowed field. The air was thick with humidity and had an electric feel to it.

Annie looked up and furrowed her brow. "Maybe we should go home."

"And leave behind all these great crawdaddies? C'mon, we'll grab some quick then get out of here."

I plopped the bucket down on the bank of the river and got on my knees, reached into the water up to my elbow and flipped over a large rock. Crawfish scuttled here and there. Annie giggled and plunged her hand into the water, pulling out two little crustaceans by their tails.

Above us the sky groaned and a few drops of water landed on my back.

"It's raining," Annie said.

"So. A little water never hurt anyone. Let's get just a few more."

Lightning flashed, thunder boomed, and it was as if the sky rolled back and a reservoir of water had been dumped on central North Carolina. Rain fell so hard and fast I could barely see Annie not two feet from me, her hair matted to her head, clothes clinging to her body.

"Ben, we gotta get out of here," she hollered.

I grabbed the bucket, now half full of squirming crawfish, with one hand and Annie's hand with the other. The river's bank had turned into a slippery, muddy slope and the water began to rush with such a fury that it seemed to have a life of its own. And it was not in a good mood.

To get to the trail leading back to the road we had to follow the bank a half mile down river then cut up a steep incline to the right.

We never made it to the incline.

Halfway there, Annie lost her footing on the bank, slipped and screamed as the river's watery claws grabbed hold of her feet. I dropped the bucket, spilling the crawfish in the mud, and tried to grab her hand with both of mine but the rain made everything so slick. Her hand slid right out of my grip and, as quickly as I could blink water from my eyes, she was gone, swept away by the furious river.

I held my breath and waited, stunned by how suddenly I'd lost her. Then, twenty feet down river, her head bobbed to the surface and she gargled my name. Panic and fear twisted her face. My heart hammered in my chest. I took off after her, my sneakers skating on the muddy bank.

Because of the sudden deluge, the water level had risen quickly, high enough that overhanging branches, which once cleared the water by four, five feet, were now within reach of someone in the water. Someone like Annie. She passed under the limb of a sycamore, groped for anything to grab hold of, and finally got her hand around a small branch. The water tore at her body, fighting terribly to pull her along, but Annie's face was tight with determination. She grunted and screamed, called my name. Within seconds I arrived, heaving wet breaths, wiping water from my face. Without hesitation, I climbed onto the limb, laid on my belly, and crawled out to where Annie had hold of the smaller branch.

The water churned and splashed below me, bubbled like it was boiling. I'll never forget the fear I saw in Annie's eyes when I reached her. We both knew if she let go it might be the end of it all for her.

Quickly, I removed the belt from my pants and looped it around my wrist, then lowered it to Annie. "Grab on like I have it and don't let go. I'll pull you in."

Annie's eyes went from the branch to the belt. "I can't." She was afraid to let go, afraid the raging water would see its opportunity and snatch her away.

"Do it quickly, Annie. You have to." I scooted forward as far as I could without losing my own grip on the limb and put the belt right next to her hand. "Take it. I won't let anything happen to you. I promise."

She did. With one hand she let go of the branch and grabbed the belt, looping it over her wrist so it locked in place.

I shimmied backward on the limb, pulling Annie with me, the water tugging her the other way. Finally, with the rain pelting us, we made it safely off the sycamore and back to the bank. Annie and I both collapsed, sucking air and letting the water run down our faces. We were crying so hard we couldn't tell what were tears and what was rain.

The two of us sat there without saying a word to each other until the rain slowed enough that we could leave.

We never did tell our parents what happened that day down by the river, but Annie and I used to talk about it frequently. She said it was the day she knew we'd be together forever because I saved her life and she owed me hers.

***

The screen door opened and closed, bringing me out of the past and back to the porch where my dad used to sit puffing on his cigar, blocking out the rest of the world.

Tom was there, hands in his pockets, shirt untucked. He'd made himself at home, which was the way Mom wanted it; it was the Southern way, after all.

"Mind if I sit a spell?" he said.

I motioned to the other rocker. "Not at all."

He sat and began rocking. The creaking of the porch boards under the weight of the chair threatened to pull me back into the land of memories, a dark land with few smiles and even fewer laughs. "Sure is good to be here, to see you again, to see Miss Lizzy. She's doin' real fine."

"Yeah, she's coming along. She's such a little trooper. She'll be off the walker soon and using crutches."

Tom nodded. "That'll be fine. Real fine."

"Then hopefully by Christmas she won't be using anything."

Tom looked at me and smiled big. "Be a good Christmas present for her."

I didn't say anything but he knew what I was thinking. It would be our first Christmas without Annie and nothing could fill the emptiness she'd left.

I wanted to change the subject. "How're things at the hospital?"

"Things are just fine. Stayin' in business."

"Hard for a hospital to go out of business, I guess. People are always gonna get sick or hurt. Is Rose still there?"

Tom's smile returned. "Rose is a sweetheart. Sometimes I think she cares too much."

I was glad to hear Rose hadn't lost her passion yet, that the stresses of the job, the pressure, the long hours, hadn't calloused her heart.

We sat there in silence for a few minutes, two friends just listening to the drums of nature playing in the distance and watching the light show being displayed somewhere miles to the west.

Finally Tom said, "And how are you doing, Ben?"

I knew he'd get around to asking it sooner or later. We hadn't had any real time to talk since I got home from the Piggly Wiggly and found him in the basement with my dad.

"Better than when we left PA." I hadn't really thought about it before he asked and hesitated to admit it, but being back in Boomer had been good for me. And Lizzy. My mom was playing a huge role in the care and loving of Lizzy and that lifted a weight from my shoulders. And Lizzy seemed to be getting along too, adjusting to her new surroundings as well as could be expected.

"But ..." He could tell there was more to be said.

I sighed, a deep sigh that felt like it came all the way from my soul. "But being here ... everything reminds me of her. Everything. Everywhere I turn, everywhere I look, everywhere I go, I can say, 'Annie and I were there, we did that, we talked about that, we used to hang out there.'"

"Memories are blessings but they can be curses too."

He didn't know how true those words were. But he did know, didn't he?

"I still think about her all the time. I remember. I dream. I daydream. I imagine her here and what she would say about different things. I hear her voice as if it were real and right next to me. I feel her touch, the way she used to brush her hand over me whenever she walked past. She couldn't pass me without touching me. She was just that kind of person. The pain has lost some of its edge, though. I think."

"It'll never completely go away," he said, and I believed him. "There will always be a part of you that mourns for her, that misses her friendship, her laugh, the way she hummed her favorite hymns when she worked in the kitchen, the smell of her perfume in the morning and how it changed its scent as the day went on." I knew he was talking about himself now, about his wife. He nodded slowly and stared at the flashing sky. "Yes, the pain will fade but it'll never go away. Not completely. You just learn to live with it. Make it a part of who you are and go on living."

"And what if you don't want to go on living?"

He looked at me and frowned. "Now where would a thought like that come from? You got Miss Lizzy to think about, to raise, to love. She needs you now more than ever before."

He was right, of course. I hadn't seriously thought about ending my life, but way back in the dark corners of my mind the thought did reside and it would show itself from time to time in the darkness of the night, when sleep eluded me and the memories were especially painful.

"What would Annie say about that? Huh?" I said.

He laughed. "I think she'd give you an earful about that."

"Two earfuls."

Tom was quiet for a few moments then asked, "And what would Annie say about your father?"

I knew the conversation would get there eventually but was in no hurry to hasten it.

When I didn't answer immediately, Tom said, "I know what you've told me about him, about your childhood." He paused and looked to be chewing something slowly, a thought perhaps. "He's not that man no more, Ben. He's got a good heart. It's tender now."

That's what I thought he'd say. "I guess Annie would tell me I need to forgive him."

"Wise words."

"She always knew the right things to say."

"So?"

Thunder rumbled across the sky and the clouds lit up from a flash of lightning. "It's not that easy. You don't know what I went through, the damage he caused."

"He's changed now—"

"Yeah, that's what I keep hearing. But how can you tell? You can't even understand what he's saying?"

Tom shook his head, not in any kind of demeaning way but in a manner that spoke of his concern for me. "The heart doesn't have to speak with words. You can see it in him if you take the time to look. There's a peace there. And pain. Lots of pain. And sorrow."

I understood what Tom was saying, really I did. But it was like re-wallpapering an old house. You can just cover up the old paper with the new stuff, but if you really want to do the job right you need to get rid of the old paper first, and that takes work, a lot of work. Forgetting the hurt and pain I'd grown up with would take time and work to forget. And it wouldn't be easy.

Rain drops landed on the sidewalk, big jobs the size of marbles, here and there at first then all at once, like God himself opened the heavens and dumped a truckload of water over Boomer, North Carolina.

Tom and I sat with silence between us for a good long while, just listening to the thumping of the rain and the growling of the heavens. At times the rain fell with such fury it appeared to be shot from the clouds, millions of watery slugs pummeling the earth.

Finally, it slowed to a steady pattering, like the drumming of fingers on a pane of glass, and Tom stood and said, "Well, 'bout time I turn in." He turned to me and smiled. "Son, in time you'll see that there are some things in the past worth holding on to—Annie's memory being one of them—and things that aren't. When you learn to tell the difference, well, I guess then you free yourself."

He turned and left, letting the screen door close quietly behind him.

Moments later my mom stuck her head out. "I'm going to bed, Ben. You okay?"

I nodded. "Yeah, I'll be in soon."

"It's nice watching the rain fall, isn't it?"

I nodded again.

She stood in the doorway, propping the screen door open with her arm, and watched the rain for a few seconds. "I like to think the rain comes when it's needed to wash away all the gunk on the earth and make it like new again."

I didn't know if she knew how profound that statement was. Sometimes my mom surprised me.

"Well," she said. "Goodnight, Ben. I love you, sweetheart."

"Love you too, Mom."

***

That night I slept on the floor in Lizzy's room so Tom could take the guest bed. As I lay there, hands behind my head, rain tapping on the windows, my mind wandered to all sorts of places. I thought of that time I almost lost Annie in the river. The look on her face when I climbed out on that limb. The trust she'd placed in me to pull her to safety. I'd promised her that I wouldn't let anything happen to her.

And I did. I let something happen. Something terrible and violent and so permanent. And so preventable. There was still a part of me that didn't want to accept that Annie's absence from our life was permanent. She wasn't coming back. Ever. I wondered how long it would take for that truth to sink in and for me to move on, to step away from this holding pattern I'd placed myself in.

And then I thought of the discussion I'd had with Tom on the porch. His words—*In time you'll see that there are some things in the past worth holding on to and things that aren't*—wandered through my mind. I wanted to forgive my dad. I knew I should, and in my heart I think I did, but my mind just couldn't forget, couldn't get over the pain he'd caused.

My mom, in her down-home wisdom, had shaken me more than she knew. Her talk about the rain washing away the earth's gunk and making it like new made so much sense.

I needed a good rain to wash over me and make me like new.

CHAPTER 23

....

THANKSGIVING FELT THE WAY Thanksgiving should, chilly with only a hint of the moisture previous days had held. It had stopped raining sometime overnight and the ground was wet and soggy. Whatever leaves had still been clinging to their branches were now on the ground, leaving the trees as bare as skeletons. Mom spent most of the morning and the whole afternoon preparing food and conjuring up some of the most wonderful aromas this world had to offer. Under the instruction of her grandma and perched atop a barstool, Lizzy helped where she could, smiling the whole time. Only when I passed and she slid me a furtive glance did I see the sadness in her eyes and she no doubt caught it in mine too. We knew what each other was thinking, and what we were missing.

Annie loved Thanksgiving and would proclaim every year that it was her favorite holiday. Christmas came in a close second but Thanksgiving always took the prize. She'd awaken early, pad downstairs in her pajamas and get the turkey in the oven, then shower and dress in her "Thanksgiving sweater," a gawdy brown knit thing with a large embroidered turkey on the front. Then she'd spend the rest of the morning in the kitchen, stirring gravy, mixing stuffing, baking, cooking, slicing, spooning, running an operation as fast-paced and organized as any Fortune 500 company. And the whole time she'd hum and sing her favorite country tunes. Lizzy, her faithful and loyal assistant, would help getting this, getting that, measuring, pouring, stirring.

And because of all that, Thanksgiving morning was my favorite time of year. It was something taken out of a *Better Homes and Gardens* magazine. The smells, the smiles, the singing, the laughing, the happy chatter between mother and daughter. I'd sit on the sofa in the den, Macy's parade on mute, and just listen to the sounds of family the way it should be. For me, there was nothing better. The Thanksgivings we'd enjoyed were so vastly different from the ones either of us had tolerated as children that it magnified the moment, almost glorified it in a sense. There was no way any other day, not even Christmas, could dethrone it.

It was a longing for all of those missing moments that I caught in my daughter's eyes. She, too, suffered with the memories, the constant reminders of the life we'd enjoyed, the family, the love, and the glue that held it all together.

Tom and I spent most of the morning replacing some rotted boards on the back porch. I had meant to get to it eventually, but since he was there and was the handy one, I thought it would be good to recruit his help. As usual, I was the one helping him, fetching the saw, his hammer, nails, measuring twice, even three times. Tom used tools as smoothly as a surgeon wields his instruments; his hands were steady and his cuts always precise. When I assisted him with anything related to carpentry I absorbed as much as I could. And while we worked he did most of the talking. He was a good talker and a great teacher. Again, I soaked up as much as my mind would hold.

Shortly after noon we finished the porch and Tom headed upstairs to shower and change. I followed my nose into the kitchen to see how the preparations were coming along. Mom was putting the finishing touches on the pecan pie before sticking it in the oven and Lizzy rolled dough. Flour dusted her nose, forehead, and cheeks. When I entered she looked up and smiled.

"Look, Dad, I'm helpin' Gammy make pies."

I looked at my mom. Gammy is what I called my grandma, my mom's mother. She and her husband lived in Tennessee and we only saw them on holidays. As far as I remembered, they were kind people, soft-spoken and tenderhearted, and they gave me lots of gifts at Christmas.

"I told her she could call me that," Mom said.

It dawned on me then that Annie and I never discussed what Lizzy would call our parents. We always referred to them as Grandma and

Grandpa but we had failed to ask what they wanted to be called.

"That's fine," I said. Then to Lizzy, "Did Gammy tell you where that name came from?"

Lizzy dragged the back of her hand across her forehead to push a few loose strands of hair to the side. "She said you used to stutter and would always get stuck on your Rs so you just started calling your grandma Gammy 'cause it was easier."

I wiped some of the flour from Lizzy's face. "That's right. So Gammy it was and it stuck." I called her that until she died. She was only sixty-five; I was fourteen.

Mom opened the oven door and slid the pie onto the middle rack. As she closed the door she said, "Why don't you go down and see if your dad's watching the game? I'm sure he'd enjoy your company."

The game was what Thanksgiving was always about to my dad. That and food and beer. Never family. I'd spent too many Thanksgivings watching him watch his precious football game to want to go down there and suffer through another one.

"I think I'll go out on the porch."

My mom frowned at me. She didn't need to say anything; her facial expression said it all.

"I don't like football, Mom. I never did. Besides, that's all ..."

I let my words trail off. Another Thanksgiving didn't have to be ruined because of what my dad did or didn't do. It was better just to let things go and keep my thoughts to myself. Lizzy didn't have to hear about what a self-indulged jerk her grandpa had been.

Mom's face grew red and her eyes welled with tears. She turned quickly toward the sink before Lizzy noticed and busied herself with washing up a few spoons and bowls.

I kissed Lizzy on the head. "If you need anything I'll be on the porch, okay kiddo?"

"Okay, Dad," she said. "Me and Gammy got it here."

"I know you do."

***

167

At three o'clock I went inside and took a shower, washed the sawdust and grime from my body, and got dressed. I found Tom and Lizzy back downstairs, setting the table in the dining room. It was a long, sturdy farm table that seated eight comfortably, ten if everyone gave up a few inches of elbow room. I don't know that my parents ever even *had* eight people at it. Growing up, we never used it because it was always just Mom and me.

The two of them had quite the system down. Tom would run between the kitchen and dining room and hand plates and silverware to Lizzy in her wheelchair. She'd then place them on the table as neatly as possible, forks on the left, knife and spoon on the right, just like Annie had taught her. Only there was one problem.

I lifted one of the plates and silverware from the table. "You have too many place settings, kiddo."

"Gammy said there would be six of us. Miss Celio is still coming, right?"

"As far as I know."

I walked into the kitchen with the plate in my hand but my mom was right there. She took the plate from me, the knife, forks, and spoon, gave me a sideways look I'd seen too many times as a kid, and walked past me back into the dining room. Replacing the extra place setting she said, "Your father is eating too."

"With us?"

She brushed past me, headed back to the kitchen.

I followed her and noticed Tom giving me a look of warning.

"Since when?" I said.

She stopped in the kitchen and turned around. Her face was red again. "Since he decided he had more to be thankful for than a good football game. He's thankful to be alive, Ben. To have a wife who loves and cares for him, to have a son who has made something of himself. He's thankful to open his home to you and Lizzy in your—" She put her hand to her mouth and turned away.

I'd blown it. Big time. And on Thanksgiving. "Mom. C'mon. I'm sorry, okay?"

Tom leaned against the counter, arms crossed, eyes on the floor.

Lizzy sat in her chair in the doorway between the kitchen and dining room and looked at me with wide, disappointed eyes. It was the same look Annie used to give me when I'd stick my foot in my mouth or act out of selfishness or just plain stupidity.

I took a step toward my mom just as a knock sounded on the front door.

Amy.

***

With the meal spread out on the table, we found our seats and licked our lips. The turkey took center stage, an eighteen-pounder cooked with herbs and sliced thin, each piece oozing the juices inside. Surrounding the turkey were bowls full of cornbread dressing, cranberry salad, and mashed potatoes, and dishes of green bean and sweet potato casseroles. There were also homemade biscuits, more than enough for everyone.

Mom sat at one end of the table and dad at the other. Lizzy and I took one side and Tom and Amy the other. When everyone was seated and settled, the aromas of the feast mingling and tempting us, my mom put her hands on her lap and cleared her throat.

"I feel blessed to be able to share this day with all of you. We all wish Annie could be here. She would have liked this, I think." She reached over and took my hand. I nodded at her. Annie would have liked it; I had no doubt about that. She was always able to make the best of any situation.

Mom continued, "Thank you, Tom and Amy, for joining us. You're very welcome here so please make yourself at home."

Tom closed his eyes and nodded and Amy smiled. She looked nice, I couldn't deny that. And in the light from the oil lamps Mom had going she looked a lot like the sixteen-year-old I dated all those years ago.

"We have much to be thankful for," Mom said. I could tell she was holding back the tears by the tightness in her voice.

But I didn't feel like giving thanks. Sure there were things to be thankful for—Lizzy's recovery was going as well as could be expected, Tom's friendship had helped us both through the deepest darkest valley imaginable, the turnaround I'd seen in my mom—but they all seemed overshadowed by the fact that my wife and the mother of my daughter had been violently torn from us, leaving a raw, open wound that promised never to fully heal. It felt like having someone beat you to within an inch of your life then tell you you should thank him for sparing your life.

Mom cleared her throat again and looked at my dad. "Walter would like to give thanks."

While everyone bowed their head, I watched my dad. I wondered how he would pray if he couldn't communicate. I also wanted to witness something I'd never seen before: Walter Flurry talk to God.

Dad folded his hands and bowed his head. His Adam's apple bobbed and brow creased. "Um, we ... uh, over it, no ... watch the ... presence." Dad stopped and wiped a hand across his forehead. He opened his eyes and lifted his head, looked around the table. When he got to me, we met eyes. A single tear spilled out of his right eye, traveled along the line of his nose, and caught on his nostril. In those gray eyes, I saw something I'd never seen before, at least not in my father. I saw humility. I almost missed it too because, just as quickly, he dropped his head and shut his eyes tight. "Pardon, uh ... no ... make better ... um, stop."

That was it. He opened his eyes again and those around the table slowly got the hint that he'd finished. I kept staring at my dad for a few seconds after everyone else had begun passing the dishes. It wasn't until I felt my mom's hand on mine that I pulled my eyes away.

"God hears his heart, Benjamin," she said softly. "He understands."

I looked back at my dad. He was smiling at Lizzy. Funny, I didn't ever remember him smiling before his stroke.

The conversation around the table was light and spontaneous. Mom did most of the talking, asking Tom about his work at the hospital and Amy about her work at the school. I was thankful that never once did I have to talk about Annie. Not that I didn't want to, goodness no. I could have written a whole volume of books about Annie and the person she was and the life we shared. But I knew if I got to talking about her the tears would want to flow and I was in no mood to hold them back.

When most of the food had been consumed and everyone had pushed a few more inches away from the table, Mom stood and asked for help clearing the plates. Tom, Lizzy, and Amy were right on it, moving back and forth between the kitchen and dining room as effortlessly as the well-trained kitchen staff at any five-star restaurant.

Mom took my arm and leaned close. "Ben, can you take your father back down to the basement? I can tell he's tired."

Dad did look tired. All the activity around dinner had depleted what limited energy stores he had. I didn't want to do it. I didn't want to be alone with him. It reminded me too much of those days when I'd take him his six-pack and sit on the floor and watch the game while he downed one beer after another and talked more to the TV than he did to his own son.

But the look on my mom's face told me to do what I'd been asked. "Sure."

I led Dad to the steps and, holding his left arm, guided him down to the basement. He walked in a clumsy manner, stiff-legged and unsteady, kind of like Frankenstein's monster in those old black-and-white movies. Without someone to steady him he'd no doubt lose his balance and tumble down the steps.

Once in his chair, Dad smiled at me and reached for my hand. I hesitated then took his offer. After a moment I tried to pull my hand away but he grabbed it with both of his and pulled me closer. Despite the stroke and his relative inactivity, he still had a grip like iron. I leaned in. "What is it, Dad?"

My dad gazed deep into my eyes but didn't say anything. Instead he tightened his lips and nodded. He didn't need to say any words to let me know what he was thinking; I could see it etched in the lines of his face, the shadows in his eyes, the tension of his jaw. He was apologizing.

"I know, Dad," I said. "But it doesn't erase the hell you put us through."

I was glad my mom wasn't there to hear me say that, but it needed to be said. He needed to hear it. Because it was true. It was one thing to apologize for damage caused, but an entirely different matter for the ones wronged to have to deal with the aftermath of that damage.

Dad nodded again and squeezed my hand harder. "I, um, show ... no, um, pressure." He shook his head. "No."

"It's okay, Dad. I understand."

He swung his head side to side. "No. I ... crow, tell ... no, uh, good." He waved his hand in front of his face as if shooing an invisible fly and shook his head in defeat. He'd tried to tell me something else but the fight with his damaged brain had exhausted and frustrated him.

I reached for the television remote and sat it on his lap. "Do you need anything else? A drink or anything?"

He shook his head and waved me off.

When I arrived back upstairs the table had been cleared, the leftovers put in separate containers and refrigerated, and the dishwasher loaded. Tom and Lizzy sat on barstools while Mom washed a pot in the sink.

Amy turned to me and smiled. "I best be getting home. My dog will be wondering where his dinner is." She held up a small container. "Your mom was kind enough to send something special home for him."

"Heart, liver, and gizzard?"

She smiled and nodded. "Yum, right?"

"Makes my mouth water just thinking about it."

Amy thanked my mom and said her goodbyes to Lizzy and Tom.

"I'll walk you out," I said.

We stopped outside on the porch and Amy faced me. She was a full eight inches shorter than me. She looked up and pushed hair off her forehead. "Thanks for inviting me, Ben. I had a real nice time."

"I'm glad you could come."

"Tom is really nice."

"Yeah, I don't know where I'd be without him. He came into our life at just the right time."

"Seems like he's been good for both of you. He gets along so well with Lizzy."

I looked past Amy at the trees lining the driveway. "Sometimes I think he knows how to help her better than I do."

She put her hand on my arm. "I'm sure you do just fine. You're a wonderful father."

My eyes went to the Fleming house next door and a twinge of guilt stabbed at me. As nonchalantly as I could, I pulled my arm away from her touch.

"I'm sorry," she said and I could tell I'd embarrassed her.

"No, don't be. You didn't do anything wrong. I just—"

"I should get going. Thanks again. And please thank your mother again. Everything was wonderful."

She turned and left. I watched as she got into her car and pulled away without looking back once, and cursed myself for being so sensitive and insensitive. I sat in the rocker, looked over at the Fleming house, and wondered what Becky was doing.

CHAPTER 24

A WEEK AFTER THANKSGIVING, LIZZY graduated from her walker to a pair of new, shiny pink Loftstrand forearm crutches. It took two therapy sessions for her to get comfortable using them and coordinate the swing of the crutches with the movements of her legs. In a matter of days, though, she was an old pro and was enjoying her freedom apart from the cumbersome walker. Also, with the transition to the crutches, the wheelchair became obsolete. To commemorate the milestone, we stuck the chair and the walker in the back of the SUV, drove them down to the Boomer United Cerebral Palsy office, and donated them. We were sure there was some kid out there in need of a nice wheelchair or walker and we were so glad Lizzy was no longer that kid.

On the way home I glanced in the rearview mirror at Lizzy in the back seat. "So how do you feel, sweetie? Finally got rid of that stuff."

She shrugged. "I dunno. They weren't that bad."

"Weren't that bad?" I feigned exasperation. "Don't you remember when you were stuck in that chair, before you were allowed to walk? You hated it. And that walker, ugh, you used to complain about it all the time."

"I know." She looked out the window. "But they kinda grew on me, you know?"

"No, I don't know." But I did. Both the wheelchair and walker represented security, something safe and predictable in my daughter's life. And she needed that. Moving away from them signified another change, another movement from one stage of life to another. It told her that she had to be more independent now. And that it was time to go back to school.

When we got home, I helped Lizzy out of the truck. Even with her crutches she still needed help up the porch steps. Her legs weren't strong enough to lift her body weight yet. Once inside she nearly threw herself on the sofa and let the crutches fall to the floor.

I sat next to her as Mom came into the room. "So how did it go?"

"She misses her walker," I said.

Lizzy laughed. "No I don't."

"You said you like it," I said, digging my elbow into her side.

She rolled her eyes. "I said it wasn't that bad, Dad."

My mom sat on the opposite side of Lizzy and stroked her hair. "You walk so beautifully with your crutches."

Suddenly Lizzy grew serious and stared at her hands, shoulders slumped.

"What's the matter?" I asked.

Lizzy lifted her shoulders and dropped them dramatically. "Do I still have to go back to school?"

"Yes, you do," I said. "And I still need to find a job. We both have things we need to do."

Lizzy glanced at her crutches on the floor. "But the other kids will still laugh at me with those things."

I took her tiny hand in both of mine. "Some of them might, sure, but who cares what they think. I talked to Mr. Grubbs and he's gonna be watching out for you. I don't think you'll have any problems this time."

If I'd known better, I would have cooked up some crow and eaten my words right then and there, saved myself the trouble of doing so later.

***

I was at the local jobs center, filling out one of those generic applications, when I got the phone call. There'd been an "altercation" at school and Lizzy was involved. Busting the speed limit by double digits, I made it across town in less than ten minutes. I had a pretty good idea that whatever kind of altercation it was, Lizzy didn't start it. My paternal instincts were in high gear. I pushed through the school office doors and walked up to the receptionist's desk.

"Is she okay?" I said. Heat crawled up my neck and settled in my cheeks.

She looked at me with wide eyes and stood. "Mr. Flurry, she's fine. Just ... well ..."

She hurried me back a short hallway to the principal's office and opened the door.

"Here," she said. "Mr. Grubbs will explain everything."

I walked in and found my daughter on a chair crying. Her eyes were red and puffy and she had a bandage on her right elbow. An older woman with dusty-gray hair knelt beside her.

I looked around the room. Mr. Kittinger, the principal, was there, as was Marty.

The look on my face must have said everything before I had a chance to open my mouth.

Marty approached me with both hands in the air like I was a robber pulling a stick-up. "It's being taken care of, Ben."

"What? What's being taken care of?" I knelt beside Lizzy and touched her arm. "Are you okay, kiddo?"

She sniffed and nodded.

"What happened to your elbow?"

Mr. Kittinger stood from his chair and motioned toward the woman beside Lizzy. "Mrs. Alvarado saw the whole thing. She was on recess duty when it happened."

"When what happened?" I looked from Lizzy to Mrs. Alavarado.

Mrs. Alvarado stood, keeping her hand on Lizzy's shoulder. "One of the boys kicked out her crutch and she fell on the blacktop."

More heat poured through my veins. I'd been bullied enough as a kid, I wasn't going to stand by and let my daughter receive the same treatment. "Which boy?"

Kittinger stepped forward. "That's already been—"

I stared at Marty. "Which boy?"

With his arms crossed, he dropped his eyes to the floor.

"It's being taken care of," Kittinger said.

Ignoring him, I went to Lizzy. "What was the boy's name, sweetie?"

She glanced around the room with teary eyes. "Daddy?"

I'd pushed too hard. Kneeling again, I wrapped my arms around my daughter. "I'm sorry, honey. I'm sorry that happened."

I heard a man's deep voice from outside the office, in the receptionist's area. The look on Marty's face said what I needed to know. I walked out of Kittinger's office in time to see a big guy in a Carhartt jacket disappear through the doorway, a boy by his side.

"Hey." I ran after him and caught up in the hallway. "Hey you."

He stopped and turned slowly. "Yeah?"

He was bigger than he looked from twenty feet away. Thick neck, barrel chest, couple day's worth of growth on his face. The kind of guy that liked to hang out at the bar on Friday night and maybe get a fight or two in before staggering home. Reminded me of my dad.

I nodded at the kid. "That your son?"

He turned to face me fully. "Yeah."

"What're you here for?"

"What's it to ya?"

"He pick on a girl? Is that why you're here?"

The big guy's eyes shifted.

"That girl was my daughter. They tell you what he did? Kicked one of her crutches out from under her?"

I was shaking like a naked squirrel in Alaska and hoped he didn't hear it in my voice.

"I'll take care of it," he said, but the tone of his voice said he couldn't care less.

"Why don't you teach your son some social skills? What kind of kid picks on a girl with crutches?"

I couldn't believe the words pouring out my mouth, formed by anger and frustration. Anger that my daughter had been bullied and hurt, and frustration because I'd been absent and once again failed to protect her.

The big guy stepped forward, so close our chests almost touched. "Why don't you mind your own business and—"

"This *is* my business," I said, pulling my shoulders back. I knew I was asking to be hit but, at the moment, I didn't care.

Two thin arms wedged between us and a woman followed them. It was Amy. "Guys, knock it off," she said. "Back off."

I stepped back, staring at the big guy, my pulse thumping in my neck so hard I thought my arteries would burst. Amy put a hand on my chest and pushed me back even farther. "Ben, go back to the office."

I did as I was told, gathered Lizzy and left without saying a word to Kittinger, Marty, Mrs. Alvarado, or anyone else. I was embarrassed and humiliated. I'd let my anger get the best of me and made a fool of myself in front of not only Amy but half the school. I held my tears back until we got home and I'd taken Lizzy inside to my mom. Then, in the woods behind my parents' home, I let the torrents come. I couldn't do this on my own. I needed Annie. She would have known exactly how to handle that situation at the school and would have pulled it off perfectly. Like a scab being knocked off, the wound was opened again and another wave of tears washed over me. I leaned against a tree and let them come, confident that no one could hear me this far in the woods.

Because of the sobs, I failed to hear the footsteps approaching.

"Hey, Ben, you okay?"

I spun around and nearly knocked Becky over. Dragging my sleeve across my eyes, I said, "What are you doing here?"

"I saw you come home with Lizzy. I just wanted to make sure everything was all right." She looked frightened, like she'd walked into a lion's den unawares and awoken the sleeping and hungry beast.

I leaned my back against the thick trunk of a towering oak. "More trouble at school."

"Marty again?"

"No. I can't keep blaming him. Some kid decided to bully her. Nothing anyone could have done about it."

"Is she okay?"

I nodded. "She's got a skinned elbow and bruised feelings, but, even worse, her dad made a complete idiot of himself."

Becky put her hands in the pockets of her jeans and tilted her head to the side to make eye contact with me. "It couldn't have been any worse than punching her teacher in the face."

For the first time all day I smiled. "You don't know who you're dealing with here." I told her what happened, how I almost got my face pushed in by a guy nearly twice my size, and how Amy, not more than five and half feet tall, had to rescue me.

Becky pulled her hands from her pockets and crossed her arms. "I think you're too hard on yourself."

"Really? I think I'm not hard enough." I sighed. "I don't know what I'm doing. I can't raise a daughter. She needs a mother, a woman. I'm a lummox."

"Isn't that a Doctor Seuss character?"

Now I full-out laughed. "That's a lorax."

"Oh. Is that better than a lummox?"

Becky was good for me. She had the same sense of humor that Annie had, the kind that could dissolve the tension in any situation.

"I think a lorax is probably better than a lummox, yeah."

"Seriously," she said. "You're too hard on yourself. You're a great dad, and, considering where you came from, that's really saying something. You'll get the hang of the girl thing. We're a different breed but not totally impossible to figure out. Right now all Lizzy needs is love and you're good at that."

Now I was the one shoving my hands in my pockets. "Thanks. You know, you remind me a lot of Annie."

"Probably because we're sisters. Sisters are like that."

"Yeah, I guess. Really, though, thanks."

"Hey, anytime you need help or want to talk or whatever I'm just right next door, okay?"

"Yeah." Annie had said those exact words to me sixteen years earlier. I had just been read the riot act by my dad after he belittled me and accused me of being ungrateful for the food he put on our table. She'd found me in the tree house tossing baseball cards against the wall and talked me out of my slump for the millionth time.

As I walked with Becky through the woods, back to the clearing where our parents' homes stood and a lifetime of memories resided, my shoulder touched hers and our hands brushed.

And I didn't feel guilty about it.

CHAPTER 25

....

I'VE NEVER LIKED GUNS. When I was ten my uncle took me to a firing range and let me shoot his Winchester .308. I hit the target almost dead center nine out of ten shots but hated every time I squeezed the trigger. The concussion, the recoil, the power behind that bullet, it all scared me. Maybe I was too young to handle the rifle, maybe I just wasn't designed for guns. In any case, for my next birthday my mom got me a Daisy pump BB gun. My dad, who owned one .12 gauge but never shot it that I know of, sneered and called it a girl's gun.

After taking the gun from its box and loading it with BBs, I tramped outside and stood at the edge of the woods. I felt like a big game hunter and pretended I was on an expedition to bring down the infamous Sasquatch. With the gun slung over my shoulder, I headed into the deep woods, senses alert, listening, smelling, watching everything.

I thought I saw something move ahead of me, from one tree to another, something big and dark and hairy. My mind spun and my heart began to hammer. It looked to walk on two legs, a lumbering stride.

Stopping behind a smooth-barked sycamore, I brought the pre-pumped gun to my shoulder and looked down the sight at where I'd seen the movement, watching, waiting for the elusive creature to show itself again.

Footsteps from behind startled me. I spun around and found Annie there, smiling mischievously. She looked at the gun, then at me. "Is that real?"

I was almost ashamed to tell her the truth. Every other kid in my grade had a rifle of his own and had taken the hunting safety course offered by the school. Owning a rifle and hunting with your dad were rites of passage for young men in Boomer. "It's a BB gun," I said, trying to sound as confident as I could.

"Oh. Did you get it for your birthday?"

"Yeah."

"Happy birthday."

"Thanks."

She glanced past me, into the woods. "Were you gonna shoot something?"

"I uh …" I wasn't about to tell her I was waiting for Sasquatch to show his furry head. "No, I was just foolin' around with it."

"Are you any good?"

"At what?"

She nodded at the gun. "Shooting?"

"Heck yeah." I turned and scanned the woods, the trees, the saplings, looking for a good target, one that would totally impress the girl next door. I spotted a nuthatch, head-down, about twenty yards away, clinging to the bark of an old oak. "Watch this," I said.

I brought the gun to my shoulder and found the bird in its sights.

It took Annie a moment to see what it was I was aiming at. "Maybe you shouldn't," she said.

I was glad she had more confidence in me than I did. Honestly, I didn't think I had a prayer of hitting that bird and was thankful, because I really didn't want to hit it. But I'd already put myself out there and now had to finish the deed. I aimed slightly high to compensate for the distance and the trajectory of the BB and slowly squeezed the trigger. The BB made a perfect flattened arc through the air and struck the nuthatch mid-back. It fell from the tree as easily as if someone had swatted it away with the back of his hand.

"Benjamin Flurry!" Annie shouted as she took off toward the fallen bird.

I followed her, and when I caught up she was holding the tiny nuthatch in her hands. It was still alive but barely. It lay motionless in her cupped hands, its little chest pumping spastically, staring at me as if to question why I'd shot it. What did it ever do to me?

Annie shot me a look of both sadness and anger.

"I ... I didn't think I'd hit it," I said.

"Well, you did. With that stupid gun of yours."

A lump lodged in my throat. I don't remember which upset me more, the fact that I'd injured—possibly, fatally—an innocent bird minding its own business or that Annie was so upset with me. Slinging the gun over my shoulder and reaching out my hands, I said, "Give it to me."

She pulled away. "What are you gonna do?"

"I'm gonna take care of it. I shot it now I need to mend it."

She stood and held the bird against her belly. "I'll carry it. Where are we going?"

"To my garage." I didn't want my mom or dad knowing what I'd done. Mom would scold me; Dad would mock me.

In the garage I found a box and Annie lined it with grass and leaves. We put the bird in the middle of our homemade nest and both sat there staring at it for a good hour.

The next morning we met at the garage before school and found the bird dead. That was my first experience shooting at anything living, but it wouldn't be my last.

***

A week before Christmas, Lizzy ran out of pain medication. I'd pulled her out of school again, intent to keep her home until after Christmas break then re-evaluate where we were at that time. My mom suggested home-schooling her. I could teach her during my down time once I found a job and Mom could help out when she was home in the late afternoon and evening. This became a very real possibility and would allow us to work through the summer so Lizzy wouldn't have to repeat first grade.

Lizzy was fully accustomed to her new Loftstrand crutches now and using them to get her everywhere. She still needed help with steps, but once she got going on a level surface she buzzed around like an ant looking for a handout. But this increase in activity also brought an increase of pain in both her legs. At night the aches would set in and keep her up well past midnight. Medication didn't eliminate the pain completely but at least cut the edge enough that Lizzy could get some sleep.

The Friday before Christmas, Lizzy was in tears. The pain was intense. I'd intended on getting the pain medication prescription refilled a few days earlier, but a terrible ice storm had paralyzed the South and had everyone homebound. Ice, an inch thick, encrusted everything, making the world look like a crystal winterland.

Lizzy looked up at me with tears coursing down her cheeks and said, "Daddy, do something, please."

And that's when I made up my mind. I turned to my mom. "I'm going out to the pharmacy to get the refill."

"But the roads, Ben. They're terrible."

"They've had some time to work on them. Maybe they won't be so bad." Lizzy was on her bed, rubbing both her legs. The sight of my daughter in pain and me once again unable to help her set my jaw and firmed my resolve. "She needs her medication."

"Daddy, don't," Lizzy pleaded. "I'll be okay."

I sat on the bed and hugged her. "I'll be fine, sweetie. I'll be careful. You stay here with Gammy and she'll get you in the bathtub." A warm bath usually helped to temporarily alleviate the aches.

Checking her watch, my mom said, "The drug store closes in a half hour."

"Plenty of time."

"Be careful," she said.

"Of course."

I ran downstairs, grabbed the keys to the SUV, and headed out into the bitter cold. It took me ten minutes to scrape the ice from the windshield, but once I did I was on the road in no time, doing twenty in a thirty-five. Outside the warmth of the vehicle's cab, the world was cold and hard. The trees glimmered in the moonlight but stood frozen in place as if the storm had hit centuries ago and the world had just stopped in place. No other vehicles were on the road.

I rolled the window down and listened to the silence. I didn't think I'd ever get used to that feeling of being alone. Occasionally, I'd pass a home set back a ways off the road, lights on in the windows, a plume of smoke rising from the chimney, but there was no life, no movement. People were tucked in behind their walls, oblivious to what was passing them by on just the other side.

The town of Boomer was usually quiet and mostly lifeless at night, but at this time there were typically folks still muddling around, kids hanging out at the McDonalds, folks going out to eat. On this particular night, though, there was only the infrequent truck, wheels turning silently on the ice-glazed streets.

Finally I arrived at Taylor's Drug and Hardware, the only pharmacy in Boomer. I had five minutes to spare. The front door opened with the beep of an electronic bell. Hank Taylor's little business was an all-purpose, one-stop store, about as good as it got for a town like Boomer. It had the pharmacy and hardware sections but also sold some groceries, household items, sporting goods, and developed photos. And Mindy Taylor, Hank's daughter, was the local notary public. If you needed something in a pinch, Hank's was the place to go.

The pharmacy was in the back of the store; you had to pass through the grocery section and a bunch of garden tools to get there. This time of year, Hank also stocked bags of rock salt, most of which had already been bought.

I rang the call bell at the counter and waited. A minute later, Hank emerged. He was in his late sixties but looked to be about ten years older than he was. His thick gray hair was usually unkempt and disheveled and his eyebrows in need of a good trimming. He had a bushy mustache that hung well below his upper lip and hid most of his mouth. Deep crevices outlined his eyes and mouth.

"Do for ya?" Hank said in a voice that had weathered an entire day and was beginning to sound a little hoarse.

I slid the pill container across the counter. "I need a refill on these."

Hank held the bottle at arm's length and studied the label through the lower half of his bifocals, then glanced at his watch. I looked at mine. We still had a couple minutes.

"You need it t'night?" he said.

"If it's possible. Lizzy's in some pain and we ran out."

"I see that." Again, he checked his watch then the bottle. "Well, all right. Stick around. Be a few minutes."

While I waited, I wandered over to the hardware section on the other side of the store. For its size, Hank's had a decent enough selection of tools and hardware. Every shelf was stocked about as full as it could get without collapsing on the one below it. Peg boards crowded with hand tools and prepackaged hardware lined the far wall.

The door chime sounded again and I checked the time. 9:03. Then, a moment later, Hank's wife Jackie hollered. "Front door's gettin' locked."

Minutes later there was a commotion at the back of the store, near the pharmacy counter. A man hollered, a woman screamed. Harsh talking followed but I couldn't make out what was being said. About seven aisles of tools, extension cords, cleaning supplies, and groceries separated me and the pharmacy, so I couldn't see what the problem was. I stepped out of the aisle and crossed into the next one, then peeked around the corner. A man was there in a heavy black coat, ski mask over his face. He held a handgun in one hand and had his other arm wrapped around a woman's neck. She pulled at his arm and struggled to free herself. The man jerked her around, cursed, then pointed the gun across the counter and yelled, "Give it to me. Now! Or she gets it."

My heart thumped like a race horse's hooves. I ducked back behind the shelving and tried to collect my thoughts. I had my cell phone in my pocket but by the time I called the police he could be gone or could've done something far worse.

I poked my head around the shelf again. The woman squirmed and this time I caught a glimpse of her face. It was Amy Celio.

Without stopping to plan or strategize, I dashed to the front end of the aisle and crossed the distance of the store. I rounded the corner of the shelves and stood still, the length of the aisle between myself and the action. The man's back was to me. Jackie stood by the pharmacy counter, hand over her mouth, but Hank was nowhere to be found.

"Shut up!" the man shouted as he knocked the barrel of the pistol against Amy's head. "Shut up or I'll blow your brains out."

Amy whimpered and stopped struggling.

Quickly, I stepped down the aisle, staying close to a shelf full of paper towels and toilet paper. I had no plan. I just knew I had to do something and would take it as it came to me. The man continued to holler at Amy, at Jackie behind the counter, and at Hank who was still out of sight. About halfway down the aisle, I broke out into a run. When I was fifteen feet from the man and Amy, my sneaker squeaked on the tile floor and he began to turn. At half turn, I connected with him. I'd never played football, but the hit I put on him would have made any coach smile.

He was as solid as he was big. But the force of my impact threw him off balance and he stumbled sideways. A gust of air escaped his lungs and Amy screamed. After that, things became a tangle of arms and legs. We wound up on the floor, his hand on my face. My heart was in my mouth and all I could think about was the gun. I didn't know if he still had it or not, if he was pointing it at my head, if the bullet would penetrate my skull and wreak havoc in my brain. An image of Lizzy flashed through my mind and I knew, no matter what happened, I had to stay alive for her. She couldn't lose two parents in the span of a few months.

We struggled on the floor for what seemed minutes but was only seconds. Neither of us said anything but there were plenty of grunts and groans. At one point I grabbed a handful of the ski mask and pulled and, for a brief moment, caught a glimpse of the big man's face and thought I recognized him.

He took a close swing but missed, his fist just grazing my head. Since there had been no sign of the gun I assumed it had been knocked loose when I connected with him. I hadn't heard it hit the floor, though. I tried to pull away from him but he had a hold of my coat. Suddenly, I stopped pulling and did something I hadn't planned, but just came to me out of instinct and years of watching professional wrestling as a kid. I head-butted him square on the nose. He hollered, cursed, and his grip loosened.

I jerked away and broke free, stumbled back, lost my balance and wound up on my back on the floor. I was in too vulnerable of a position and heard him scrambling to get his feet under him. To my left something caught my attention. There, within arm's reach, was the pistol, under the rack of birth control items. I didn't know what kind of handgun it was, I just knew that when I reached for it and took it in my hand it was big, black, and weighed more than I thought it would.

The big guy was now on his feet and coming at me, hate in his eyes, grunting like a wildebeest. I swung the gun around, pointed it at him, and, just as I squeezed the trigger, an image of the little nuthatch perched upside down on the bark of that old oak flashed through my head. The gun discharged, recoiled, and flipped right out of my hands.

For an instant, everything stopped and silence prevailed. Then, as if some weird time delay had occurred, the man squealed, spun around, and dropped to the floor with a loose thud.

I sat there on my butt, shaking like a leaf in autumn. My mouth went dry as cotton and something slippery squirmed in my stomach. Amy stood not ten feet away, wide-eyed, her face colorless. Across the store, the front door rattled and someone knocked on the glass. Jackie began to whimper and cry as she rounded the counter and headed for the doors, key in hand. The man moved on the floor and groaned. I realized I had been holding my breath and exhaled.

I thought I'd gone and killed him.

Seconds later, Scotty Herald, Boomer's cop on duty, came running down the aisle. He looked at the guy on the floor, now holding his side and writhing, then at me. His eyes scanned the floor until they found the gun.

It didn't take a Sherlock Holmes to figure out what had happened. He looked at me. "You stay there, Ben." Then he got on his radio and called for an ambulance. Scotty and I grew up not five miles from each other. He was only four years younger than me but looked like he wasn't more than seventeen or eighteen. With his red hair and freckles, he was Boomer's version of Opie Taylor.

Twenty minutes later the gunman was on his way to the hospital and three other cops, all North Carolina State Troopers who had arrived shortly after Scotty, were still busy interviewing the Taylors and Amy. After finishing a phone call, Scotty approached me, thumbs tucked into his utility belt. "Ben, I'm gonna have to take you down to the station."

"Am I under arrest?"

"No. We just need more information and this isn't the place for it."

I followed Scotty outside. "Can I follow you there in my car?"

He shrugged. "Sure."

On the way to the station, I called my mom, told her I was okay but that I'd be a little late. I didn't tell her I'd shot a man.

***

The Boomer police station was a small brick building situated between Lisa's Flowers and Look Your Best, a dry cleaner. It was a mere three blocks from Taylor's Drug and Hardware and just a block off the town square.

Inside, the furniture was wooden and well used. I was taken to a small room that housed one wooden table and four chairs. Scotty told me he'd be back in a few minutes, then left and shut the door. One wall was covered with posters warning of the hazards of smoking and texting while driving, drinking and driving, and participating in illegal drug use. The other three walls were empty, the plaster nicked and scuffed and dented in one area about knee-height. Sitting there made me feel like I'd done something wrong.

After ten minutes, I got up and paced around the table. I thought about sticking my head out of the room and seeing if anyone was around or if they'd forgotten about me and gone home. Another five minutes passed and finally the door opened, but it wasn't Scotty Herald who came in. It was Marty Grubbs.

"What are you doing here?" I said.

He left the door open and leaned against the jamb. "I could ask you the same thing."

"I shot a man."

"So I heard."

My face must have been a question mark.

"Amy called me and told me what happened," he said.

"Nice to see the network of information in Boomer still works."

"She was concerned," Marty said. He pushed away from the jamb and took a step into the room. "She overheard you telling Scotty about Lizzy's medicine." He reached into his coat pocket and retrieved Lizzy's pill container, filled with the little white tablets, and put it on the table in front of me.

I picked up the container and examined the label. "I'm missing something here."

"You can go home," he said. "Amy got the pills for you from Hank. He already had everything ready to go when Kyle broke in."

"Kyle?" The familiar face behind the ski mask.

"You remember Kyle McCrady? He would have been a year older than you. Quit school when he was in eleventh grade."

I did remember. "Quiet guy, always seemed distant and distracted, like he was in his own world where people didn't exist."

"That's Kyle. He was looking for some Oxycontin he could sell on the street. He's had a few rough years."

"How is he?"

"He'll live. You caught him in the left shoulder, just below the collar bone. He'll need surgery but the recovery time will probably be the best thing for him. Keep him off the street and out of trouble for a while."

"What, are you a cop too?" I said.

Marty laughed. "No, the chief is my brother. That's why Amy called me. I talked to him and he said you can go home, get Lizzy her meds, and he'll call you in the morning."

I stood, pocketed the pill container, and shook his hand. "Thanks, Marty."

"Thank Amy."

Outside, the air bit at my face and vapor clouds formed with each breath I took. The temperature had dropped again but at least the sky was clear and there was no threat of more ice. I walked around to the side of the building and found Amy there, waiting by her car.

"Hey," she said. Her eyes were still red and swollen from crying. She walked my way and, without hesitation, wrapped her arms around my waist and leaned her head against my chest. Then she lifted her face and kissed me on the cheek. "You quite possibly saved my life, you know that, don't you?"

I thought of pulling Annie out of that rushing river, the water grabbing at her legs, tugging her back in.

"I doubt Kyle would have done anything that rash," I said. Amy had aroused something inside me. I didn't know whether it was the closeness of her body, the sweetness of her breath, the touch of her lips on my cheek, or the vulnerability in her eyes, but something about that moment had me longing for female attention and the touch of a woman.

"You never know what someone like that will do." Raising herself up on her toes so her face was only inches from mine, she said, "Have you noticed how fate keeps pushing us together?"

"I haven't been keeping track."

"Maybe you should pay closer attention." She put her lips against mine and kissed me. It was nothing passionate or earth-shattering, just a tender, gentle kiss, and then it was done. She pulled away and stepped back, put her hands in her pockets. "Thanks for showing up when you did tonight. If you weren't there it could have been a totally different ending."

I knew what she meant. That she wasn't referring to Kyle and his drug hold-up and me shooting him. She was talking about the kiss.

She lifted a hand. "See you around."

I waved back. "Bye," I said, then stood and watched her get into her car and leave.

Only after she pulled away did I notice my mouth was still open and my heart was still racing. Her kiss had affected me in a way I wasn't ready for. I didn't know how to feel about it.

On the drive back to my parents' house, the guilt struck. I had no right to kiss another woman. But I didn't kiss her, not technically; she kissed me. Still, I'd done nothing to pull away or avoid her kiss. And I couldn't deny that I'd enjoyed it.

By the time I got home Lizzy was in bed, my mom curled up next to her, rubbing her legs slowly. I gave her a pill with some water and told my mom I'd had some trouble with the roads and it took me way longer than I thought it would. I'd explain the truth to her in the morning.

After Lizzy was asleep, I grabbed a blanket and went outside to sit on the porch in the dark. I needed the fresh, cold air in my lungs, needed to clear my head. Unfortunately, the chill in the air did nothing to cool the guilt that burned in my chest. I felt like I had to confess something or apologize but there was no one to apologize to. The fact was, I'd done nothing wrong. I was a single man. As much as I hated how that sounded in my head and as much as I didn't want to admit it ... well, there it was and I couldn't hide from the truth.

Across the yards, I heard Roy Fleming hollering and cursing. Their back door opened. Becky rushed out and stopped at the edge of the porch. She put her hand to her face and I could tell she was crying. I'd seen Annie do that exact same thing too many times, and it hurt to see he was still at it. I wanted to go to her, to hold her, to tell her he didn't mean anything, that his words were empty and impotent. I wanted to comfort her like I'd comforted Annie so many times before. But I decided against it. I'd dealt with enough guilt for one night.

CHAPTER 26

CHRISTMAS MORNING CAME AND went in a blur. It seemed like before it even got started, it was already over and Lizzy was sitting in her pile of gifts like the ghost of Christmas present, smiling wide and filled to the ears with Christmas spirit. My mom had gone overboard with the presents. I had no idea she'd bought and wrapped so many. Dad joined us too. He sat in a chair in the living room and didn't say a word the whole time, but he had a smile as wide as the Mississippi stretched across his face. I'd never seen him looking so happy, so content.

When all the paper had been cleaned up and thrown away Mom announced that she was making hot chocolate and cinnamon buns for everyone.

I followed her into the kitchen and said, "Mom, you didn't have to get her so much."

"I know," she said. After filling the kettle with water, she placed it on the stove and turned the knob. The igniter clicked several times before a blue flame lit the gas. "I wanted to." She turned to me and smiled. "Really, your father wanted to."

While she retrieved the hot chocolate from the pantry and the milk from the fridge, she said, "He felt like we'd missed so many of her Christmases, we had a lot of catching up to do."

Sometimes I wondered if she put words in my dad's mouth or interpreted his mumblings to mean what she wanted them to mean.

She stopped, holding the milk chest high, and gave me a look that said she could read my mind. I'd seen those eyes so many times as a kid I no longer questioned whether she really did possess some extrasensory abilities or could just pull a bluff that would trip up even the best poker players. "And I couldn't disagree with him," she said, still eyeing me. "Now go enjoy her new things. She's excited about them."

I kissed her on the cheek. Something I'd rarely done as a teen and hadn't done since returning to North Carolina. The smile on her face told me I'd given her the best Christmas present ever. "Thanks, Mom. For everything."

Tears pooled in her eyes. She shooed me out and sniffed. "You're welcome. Now go. I'll bring the cocoa out when it's ready."

I found Lizzy on the living room floor propped against the sofa, looking at one of the gifts I'd given her. A small photo album filled with pictures of her and Annie, from the day Lizzy was born to the last day the two of them had spent together. That first day of school.

I sat on the floor next to her and looked over her shoulder. She was studying a photo I'd taken last year. We'd visited the Philadelphia Zoo, and she and Annie were fascinated by the chimpanzees. I'd snapped a picture of the two of them laughing, heads together, while a chimpanzee picked its nose in the background.

"That was fun, wasn't it?" I said.

She didn't take her eyes off the photo. "The zoo?"

"Yeah."

"It was always fun."

I knew what she meant and sometimes the wisdom my daughter showed, the depth to which her first-grade mind pondered things, amazed me. "Mom made things fun, didn't she?"

Lizzy nodded. "She was always smiling and that made everyone around her smile. We don't smile so much anymore."

It was true. Annie told me once that, compared to the life she'd had as a child, our life together, especially after Lizzy came along, was pure enjoyment from the time she woke to the time she fell asleep at night. I never told her she was wrong, though. That she even smiled in her sleep. "I guess she had a way about her, huh?" I said.

Lizzy was quiet for a few moments. She flipped through a couple more pictures then stopped on one taken during our last Christmas together. In it, she held up an American Girl doll we'd gotten her, and Annie had her arm around Lizzy's shoulders. Lizzy put her finger on Annie's face. "Dad, I wish Mom was here. She would have loved this Christmas."

The lump that so easily appeared was in my throat again. "She would have."

"Can people in heaven see us?"

I had no idea but had wondered the same thing myself so many times. Could Annie see us? Did she hear my ramblings when I stood by her grave? Did she hear my crying in the shower? Could she watch her daughter grow up?

"I think they probably can," I said, putting my arm around her and kissing her on the head. "And I know she's so excited for you right now."

Lizzy reached for the doll my mom had given her and stroked its hair. "I bet she just loves Samantha. Mom always liked American Girl stuff."

"She used to like playing with your dolls as much as you did."

Lizzy giggled. "Sometimes more than me, I think."

I kissed my daughter on the head again. "She loved having a daughter."

"I was kinda like Mom's doll, huh?"

"Sort of. She liked to dress you up and fix your hair and have tea parties with you."

She ran her thumb over the doll's face. "I remember those tea parties. They were fun. Can we have a tea party sometime?"

"Absolutely, kiddo. I make a mean cup of tea and we can use Gammy's fancy teacups."

I heard a sniff behind me. After kissing Lizzy again on the head, I stood and glanced at my dad. Tears made tinsel tracks down his cheeks. He nodded at me and half smiled. I saw two things then that I'd never seen before. One, my dad full-out cry. He'd always been as hard and emotionless as a slab of rock. And two, pride. Not pride in himself or some stubborn brand of pride; I'd seen that my whole life. But pride in me, his son, the boy he raised no matter how twisted the raising had been.

My dad was proud of me.

That night, I tucked Lizzy into bed with a stuffed bear I'd given her. Samantha, her new doll, sat on the chair beside the bed.

Lizzy squeezed the bear and smiled. "I named him Harrison."

"Harrison? Why's that?"

She looked at me as if I'd just asked her why an orange was called an orange. "'Cause he looks like a Harrison. And he likes that name."

"Oh. Well, he does look like a Harrison. It's a very fitting name."

I pulled the covers up to her chin and tucked them in around her arms and legs. Then I sat on the bed next to her. "There, all tucked in like a burrito."

"I like when you do that."

"Mom used to do that, didn't she?"

"When it was cold outside."

"She used to call you a Lizzy burrito."

"Yep."

Lizzy hugged Harrison again, then stared at the ceiling. Behind her thick blonde hair, I could see the wheels of thought turning. Finally, keeping her eyes on the ceiling, she said, "Dad, are you still married to Mommy?"

I knew she'd question that sooner or later, but I was hoping it would be later. Much later.

I ran my fingers through her hair. "Well, that's a tough question to answer. In my heart I am. But, technically ... well, when Mommy and I got married we each took a vow—"

"What's a vow?"

"It's a promise."

"So you made a promise to each other?"

"We sure did. We promised to love only each other no matter what, even when we got upset with each other, even when we got sick, even when we were miles apart. But at the end of the promise, we said 'til death do us part.'"

"What does that mean?"

"It means you promise to love only each other and stay married no matter what until one of you dies."

"And then it's over?"

"Technically. But it's not that easy in your heart."

Now her eyes met mine. "In your heart you'll always be married to Mommy."

"That's right. Annie Flurry will always be my wife."

"Does she stop being my mom too?"

I leaned in and got real close to her face, close enough to see where two freckles met and formed one large one. "Absolutely *not*. She's your mom and that's the way it will always be. Annie Flurry will always be your mother."

Lizzy ran her hand over the bear's fur and searched my eyes as if looking for an answer she didn't know the question to.

"What is it, sweetheart?"

She hesitated but kept her eyes fixed on mine. Whatever she was about to ask she wanted to watch my eyes to see if in them she found the truth. "Do you think you'll ever get married again?"

"Well, to get married I'd have to fall in love with someone else, and right now I'm still too in love with your mom to even think about that."

But I had thought about it. Not the falling in love part and not the getting married part but the part where Lizzy grows up with a mother to guide her through life as a young girl, and then a young lady, and finally a woman. I didn't know what I was doing; I was a lummox groping around in the dark, tripping over stuff, running into things.

I touched the tip of Lizzy's nose. "How about if you concentrate on being the best Elizabeth Flurry you can be and let me worry about that, okay?"

"Okay," she said. "But if you do get married again, it has to be someone just like Mommy."

Tears pushed behind my eyes. "I wouldn't have it any other way."

CHAPTER 27

ARLY JANUARY BROUGHT A warm front like North Carolina hadn't seen in decades. With temperatures pushing into the seventies, Mom opened the windows and put the screens down. Fresh, warm air blew in and stirred the dust that the furnace had been blowing around for two months. The Christmas tree was still up, still decorated, and still lit eighteen hours a day. Mom kept it up as long as she could, always did. I remember some years the tree remained in our living room until February. Finally, Dad would throw a fit, grab it with one hand, drag it through the house, dropping needles like rain, and toss it out onto the front porch, ornaments and all. It was one tantrum of his Mom didn't seem to mind. She told me once that she'd happily put up with his outburst if it meant she could enjoy Christmas for a month longer. Mom loved Christmas, I think because it was a time of peace and joy and togetherness. Maybe not in our home but the idea was there, the feeling, the spirit, and that was all she needed to transport herself to another location emotionally. Taking down the decorations, burning the tree, boxing up the ornaments all meant that the time had come to an end yet again and it was back to the daily monotony for another ten months.

That night, after tucking Lizzy into bed, I went back downstairs and joined my mom in the living room. She enjoyed the stillness of the house late at night. She'd turn off every light except the tree and sit on the sofa and stare at the lights for hours. Crossing the living room floor, I could hear pine needles dropping from their branches and landing softly on the hardwood flooring. I sat in a chair directly across from the tree without saying a word. Mom still had the windows open and a cool breeze blew against the back of my neck.

Finally, I said, "You think the tree will make it to February this year?"

Mom shook her head slowly. Her eyes never left the tree. It was as if she'd been transfixed by the spirit of Christmas, her soul held captive to the idea of some perfect Christmas land that existed only in one's imagination. "The warm weather is drying it out quicker," she said. "But I'm gonna leave it up anyway." She pulled her eyes from the tree and looked at me. "I don't want this Christmas to end."

Mom never got to spoil anyone at Christmas because my dad wouldn't let her. Finally, she'd had a Christmas where she could spoil her granddaughter and she didn't want to see it come to a close. I could understand that. "There won't be any needles left come February."

"I don't care," she said. "The lights will still be there. And the ornaments."

"And the memories?"

She paused, glanced at the tree then back at me. "I never got to celebrate Christmas the way I wanted to when you were a child."

"Dad wouldn't let you."

"He thought it was a bunch of hype. A waste of money. His family never did anything special for Christmas when he was growing up. Some years he didn't even get any presents."

The more time I spent with my mom the more complete my picture of my dad got; the more I understood why he was the way he was. But, in my mind, it still didn't excuse his behavior. As I'd reminded my mom before, I grew up under similar circumstances and didn't become a tyrannical, self-absorbed drunk. I made a choice not to. I wanted to be better than that. But it was a nice evening and the feel of Christmas still lingered in the air, and I didn't want to ruin it by getting into an argument with my mom. "This was the first time you got to do Christmas your way, wasn't it?"

She nodded and by the light of the tree I could see tears in her eyes. "It was almost perfect."

"Almost?"

"If Annie was here, then it would have been perfect."

A wave of guilt washed over me as suddenly as a tsunami overtakes a small coastal village. "Mom, I'm sorry we never came down before."

"Or we could have come to your house." There was no condemnation in her voice, my mom wasn't like that, only pain. I would have rather had the condemnation.

"I know. I'm sorry." Fact was, I simply had no attachment to my old home, to Boomer, or to my parents. There was no desire to go home for the holidays. Home was where Annie and Lizzy were and we'd made our own traditions, our own memories.

We both sat in silence then, mesmerized by the tree and its lights and sparkling ornaments. The guilt ate away at me like some flesh-consuming bacteria. Not because we'd never gone back to North Carolina for Christmas or invited my parents to Pennsylvania—not after the childhood I'd had—but because I never gave my parents another chance. I'd harbored such resentment, such anger and pain, toward them that the thought of reconciliation never even crossed my mind.

Eventually, somewhere around midnight, I got up and kissed my mom on the cheek. "I'm going to bed, Mom. I love you."

She grabbed my hand and stopped me. "Ben, I don't blame you, you know. Goodness, how could I? You and Annie were so happy. We were so proud of both of you for getting away from all this and making things right for yourself. Just know that."

I forced a smile and nodded. "Thanks, Mom. Goodnight."

I went upstairs and lay on the bed in my old room, staring at the ceiling like I'd done so many times as a kid. My dad being proud of me for anything was such a foreign concept, I didn't even know what to do with it. All my life I'd wanted him to be proud of me; it was an elusive goal that was always miles out of reach, like standing at the foot of Mt. Everest with no climbing gear, no guide, and no experience, but all the desire in the world. Finally, my eyes grew heavy and the ceiling blurred and I drifted to sleep.

***

I awoke sometime in the night with the smell of burning wood in my nose. Rolling over, I lifted my head and found the clock. It was a little after two. Had the temperature dropped that much that my mom had started a fire in the fireplace? And what was she still doing up at two a.m.? I pushed off the covers, swung my legs over the edge of the bed, and sat up. That's when I noticed the thin film of haze in the air. I crossed the room in two steps and threw open the door. Smoke poured up the stairway like water, flowing uphill and into the rooms. I heard Lizzy cough and let out a hoarse scream. She called my name. I dashed across the hall and into Lizzy's room. She was on the floor. Smoke, thick and black, hovered above her. Pulling the collar of my T-shirt up over my nose, I ran to her and lifted her into my arms. She coughed again, a terrible hack, and buried her face in my shoulder.

"It's okay, baby," I said, carrying her out of the room. "We'll be okay."

"Where's Gammy?"

My mom. She must have been in her bedroom.

I could see the flickering light of fire on the first floor illuminating the smoke. We didn't have much time. The house was old and the timber dry. It wouldn't take long for it to be totally consumed.

"Hold on," I told Lizzy. We turned around and hustled to my mom's bedroom. The door was closed so I kicked it open. Inside there was little smoke, only the haze that had been in my room. But my mom wasn't there.

"Mom!"

When no answer came, I hurried back out into the hallway where the smoke had thickened even more. It roiled and creeped like it had a life of its own.

"Hang on, baby girl." Holding Lizzy with one arm, I grabbed the railing with the other and ran down the steps, skipping two at a time.

At the bottom, I scanned the first floor. Smoke, thick and chalky, filled the upper half of the entire area. Fire blazed in the living room, the tree an inferno. Furniture was also consumed, a chair and bookcase. It was spreading fast.

From somewhere in the smoke, I heard my mom yell my name, and I moved forward, directly toward the fire.

"Lizzy, keep your face against me. Try not to breathe too deeply."

She cupped her hands around her face and pressed it more firmly into my shoulder.

I coughed violently, struggling to find oxygen in the smoke. Lizzy coughed and hacked.

The deeper we got into the living room, the more intense the heat grew. My mom called my name again and I could tell it was coming from the direction of the sofa on the other side of the room. Pressing forward blindly, keeping as low as I could without dropping Lizzy, I followed the floor to where the sofa was and found my mom on the floor, crawling toward us.

I grabbed her hand and lifted her to her feet. She coughed loudly, a wheezing, raspy hack that sounded like it was squeezing through a straw. "Mom, we gotta move."

Her legs gave out and she collapsed to the floor. "I ..."

Lizzy lifted her face. "Gammy!"

"Lizzy," I hollered. "Hide your face." I didn't want her breathing in too much smoke. Her little lungs couldn't handle as much as mine.

Eyes wide, my mom strained for air, but all she could produce was that raspy cough. I needed to get her outside into the fresh air. Grabbing her by the wrist, I groaned as I dragged her across the floor and into the hallway. At the front door, I let go and threw the door open. Cool, clean air rushed in and momentarily pushed back the smoke, but, just as quickly, the smoke changed directions and found its way out of the house. Behind us the fire roared as if it were a living beast, awakened and angry. Taking my mom by the wrist again, I dragged her over the threshold and onto the porch.

Becky was there, running across the lawn, followed by her father. They came up onto the porch.

"My mom's calling 911," Becky said. She was barefoot and in a T-shirt and pajama pants. Her dad was still in his slippers and robe.

I handed Lizzy to Becky and lifted my mom's head. Her face was black with smoke and her nose as red as a cherry. She coughed, wheezed, coughed again. "Your ..." Another cough wracked her body. "Father."

My dad was still in there, in the basement where he slept. I turned to Mr. Fleming. "Get her off the porch. I need to get my dad."

"Wait for the fire truck," he said.

But the look on my mom's face and the growing fire inside said there wasn't time to wait. I had to go now or never.

I looked back at Becky, who stood twenty feet from the porch holding Lizzy, and for an instant thought I was looking at Annie. But it wasn't Annie. Annie was gone and I couldn't lose another family member if I had it within my power to save him. My eyes met Becky's and, in hers, I saw concern. But there was more too, something else. She didn't want to lose me. And I didn't want to lose her.

I turned to enter the house and heard Lizzy call my name. But there was no time to console her. Becky would have to do that. Crossing back into the house, I covered my mouth and nose with my shirt and promised myself I wouldn't leave Lizzy. She couldn't lose another parent. Inside, the smoke had turned thicker and blacker. It surrounded me like a blanket and blinded my path. But I knew the layout of the house with my eyes closed and easily found my way to the basement steps. There was no relief there. Smoke boiled up the steps, clinging to the ceiling like it had claws. I choked, coughed, sputtered, pulled the shirt up farther around my nose. My eyes burned.

Staying low and taking the steps two, three at a time, I rushed to the basement level and over to where my dad slept in his recliner. Mom told me they'd tried a bed but he had too difficult a time getting out of it to use the bedside commode in the night. In the corner of the basement, by the washer and dryer and fuse box, flames flickered and licked angrily at the ceiling, eating away at the suspended tiles. My dad was in his chair, head lulled to one side. He'd already become overwhelmed by the smoke and lost consciousness. I slapped his cheek trying to rouse him, but it was useless.

The fire inched closer along the ceiling and part of the plasterboard had already collapsed onto the washer. The fire must have started in the fuse box and sent a surge through the house, sparking near the tree upstairs and setting it ablaze.

Again, I slapped my dad's cheek and shook his shoulders but he was as limp as a stuffed doll. I pulled at his arms to lift him but his weight was much more than I could handle. I noticed his recliner was a mechanical lift chair. The control pad was tucked in next to him but, without electricity, none of the buttons worked. The coughing hit me again and violently this time. I hacked so hard I thought I'd vomit. We needed to get out of that basement or neither of us would ever breathe fresh air again. I couldn't allow that to happen. I wouldn't. I wasn't about to let my mom lose her husband, not after all she'd put up with and all she'd finally gained. And I refused to leave Lizzy. And Becky.

I needed to do this, not only for everyone else, but for my dad. He deserved to live. Didn't he? With smoke and flames surrounding us, I found myself hesitating, wondering if I should risk my life for a man who had done nothing to encourage or inspire or even love me. He'd given me nothing and now I was being asked by fate (by God?) to give him everything. Fortunately, my decision didn't take long. Yes, he did deserve to live. It was time to bury my resentment, to leave the past where it rightfully belonged, in the past.

Grabbing a fistful of his shirt with one hand and his sweats with the other, I leaned back and strained to roll him over. Dad had always been a big guy, and sitting in that recliner hadn't done much to make him any smaller. He was easily two-hundred-plus pounds. When I got him to his side I rolled him a little more and squatted beneath him, pulling the weight of his body onto my shoulder. It took every ounce of strength I could muster to get my feet under me and stand. I stumbled to the steps, my dad slung over my shoulder, holding his legs against my chest with one hand and using my free hand to pull both of us up. But the higher we got, the more my lungs heaved and the more smoke I inhaled. Sweat poured from my brow and stung my eyes. Smoke blinded me.

Finally, the top step came. The moment my foot hit the kitchen floor, I heard the sirens wailing in the distance. I forced my legs to move, pushing forward through the hallway, where the flames lashed out and singed my arm, to the front door where both Becky and her dad met me. Carefully, all three of us carried my dad down the steps and dropped his body onto the front lawn. I collapsed next to him and rolled onto my stomach, coughing, gagging, wheezing. The world spun around me until all went black and all I could hear was Annie's voice: "It's okay, you're safe. I won't let anything happen to you. I'm not going to leave you."

CHAPTER 28

AWOKE IN A HOSPITAL room for only the second time in my adult life. The first time I'd lost my wife, this time I feared I'd lost everything else. The lights were dimmed in the room but still too bright for my sensitive and smoke-burned eyes. The last memory I had before blacking out was still fresh in my mind as if I'd never lost consciousness but merely blinked and found myself transported from the ground outside my parents' burning home to the safety and comfort of a hospital bed. It was Annie's voice, telling me everything was going to be okay, that she wouldn't leave me, not again.

I lifted a hand to shield my eyes and noticed the IVs snaking around my arm. I also had a nasal cannula pumping oxygen into my nose.

"Hey, you're awake." It was Annie's voice again. My mind swam in a sea of confusion. How ...?

I turned and found Becky by my bed, her hair pulled back off her forehead just like Annie used to do. She put her hand on my shoulder. "How do you feel?"

I looked around the room and saw that we were alone. "Where's Lizzy?"

Becky patted my shoulder. "She's fine. Your mom took her to the cafeteria."

"Mom's okay too?"

"Yeah. She sucked in a lot of smoke but she's fine."

"And my dad?"

Becky paused just long enough to allow a seed of dread to be planted. Not again. My chest tightened and throat constricted.

"He's in the ICU. He took in a lot of smoke, which cut off oxygen to his brain. There's still a lot of questions."

"About what?"

"How much function he'll recover."

I sat up and pulled off the cannula.

"Ben, what are you doing?" Becky put a hand on my chest.

"I need to see him."

"But—"

"Becky, don't try to stop me. I don't need this stuff." Besides a splitting headache I felt fine. My hands were still stained with soot from the fire and the taste of smoke was in my mouth. I untapped the IV on the back of my hand and pulled it, with the catheter, from my skin.

"Ben, you can't just—"

Swinging my legs over the edge of the bed, I said, "Where're my clothes?"

"Ben—"

"Becky, where are my clothes?"

Reluctantly, she stood and crossed the room, retrieved a duffel bag, and handed it to me. "I bought you new clothes."

"How long have I been out?"

"A day."

I took the bag from her. "Thanks."

In the bathroom, I washed the chalky soot from my face and wetted my hair. Once I had changed, I left the room and found Dad in the ICU. His skin was charred and black, blistered in areas around his face and along his arms. His eyes were mere slits from the swelling. He looked small and helpless. Frail.

Memories of Lizzy in a similar room back in Pennsylvania tortured me. Here I was again, full circle, back in the ICU, standing over the bed of someone I'd put there. Because I was certain the hatred I'd harbored for my dad, the resentment, the unwillingness to forgive, had played a role in how he got there. In ways I hadn't even fathomed, I'd become more like him than I knew. It was just that the pain I'd inflicted came in a different package.

A storm welled and boiled inside me. A range of emotions, each competing for center stage. Anger, resentment, regret; they were all there. Scratching, clawing at my soul. All at once, I wanted to curse my dad for a lifetime of torment. I wanted to blame him for every hurtful thing that had ever happened to me, including Annie's death. All at once, I wanted to fall on him, hold him, beg him to forgive me.

I stared at him in that bed until I could take it no more, until I thought I'd burst if I didn't get out of that room, out of that hospital.

Tears filled my eyes as I turned to leave the room. I passed Becky at the door. "Tell Lizzy I'm okay. I'll be back in a couple hours."

Becky followed me. "She'll be worried about you."

"Tell her there's nothing to worry about. I'm okay."

"She's been waiting for you to wake up."

I stopped and turned around. Becky looked up at me with wide, fearful eyes. For a moment I had the urge to take in her my arms and hold her. I needed her, more than I thought I did. "Please, Becky. Help me out here. I'll be back in a couple hours."

"Where are you going?"

"There's something I need to do."

"We could come with you."

"I need to do it alone."

I put my hand on her face and let it linger there until she nodded slowly.

She reached into her pocket and handed me the keys to my SUV. "Your mom and I brought it here. They were going to release you today anyway if you were doing okay."

Taking the keys, I put them in my pocket. "I'm okay."

Then I turned and left and headed to the only place I could think of that would bring me the cleansing I sought.

***

When I went outside, I was surprised by how warm it still was. Temperatures had to be in the upper sixties or low seventies. If Becky hadn't told me I'd only been out of it for a day, I would have thought I'd pulled a Rip Van Winkle and slept for three months, waking up in early April. But the dried grass and barren trees gave it away. Old Man Winter was only taking a reprieve and would no doubt reawaken with thoughts of frost and ice and maybe even snow. He wasn't finished with us yet.

As I drove, my mind went to my father and all the times as a kid I'd escaped to my room, hating him, wishing him out of my life, wishing me out of his. I had no connection to him, felt no love. I'd distanced myself so fully that I'd purposefully inserted a gulf the size of the Grand Canyon between us. It was my only way of surviving with my sanity intact. But now that things had changed, now that *he* had changed, I'd refused to bridge that gap, to extend forgiveness, to reach out to him in peace. Then my mind went to Pastor Flowers and those tent meetings we'd attended all those years ago. It surprised me that I still remembered them so well, remembered him so well. The way his face reddened and sweat poured from his forehead. The way he'd pull a folded handkerchief from his pocket and wipe it across his face, always in a counterclockwise motion. But, more importantly, I remembered so many of the words he spoke. As an impressionable kid I must have buried them somewhere in my mind, there to be retrieved later in life when I needed to hear them most. Pastor Flowers' favorite topic was the gulf that existed between God and man. It was an impassable valley, impossible to bridge from man's side. Man placed it there with his sin but only God could cover the distance between the two, and he did so with his son. Jesus made the first move; he took the initiative and brought reconciliation. Flowers used to holler and pace back and forth, sometimes with tears streaming down his cheeks, as he recalled how Jesus took to the cross willingly to die for man's sin and to bridge the gaping hole between us and God.

I was pulled out of my memories by the raindrops that plinked on the windshield. First here and there, just a few at a time, then more steadily.

Guilt hit me then like never before. If Jesus could do so much for me, why was I so unwilling to do even a fraction of that for my dad? I was a hypocrite, a hard-hearted, stubborn, selfish fool. I'd been so wrapped up in my own sorrow, my own hurt, my own pity that I neglected to see the opportunities God had placed right in front of me. The opportunity to extend forgiveness, to bring healing, to be an example for Lizzy.

After parking the SUV in the small gravel lot just off the road, I killed the engine and made the climb to the top of Deadman's Rock. I was out of breath and weak in the legs by the time I reached the top. I walked to the precipice and looked down at the Cape Fear River sixty feet below. Sweat ran down my face and dripped from my nose and chin. My heart beat like thunder in my chest; I could feel my pulse in my ears. My palms turned sweaty. I knew what I'd come to do, but was having second thoughts. It was such a long drop. The rain had picked up some too, reminding me of that time I'd almost lost Annie in those very same waters.

But I needed to do this, for myself, for Lizzy, for Dad and Mom.

I closed my eyes and whispered a prayer: "Lord, be with me." Opening my eyes, I pushed away from the ledge and fell the six stories to the river below. Hitting the water took my breath away. As if the impact wasn't shocking enough, the temperature of the water was what it should be in January, despite how the air felt. I plunged deep and, surrounded by the muddy, churning water, was momentarily disoriented. For a second I relaxed every muscle in my body and allowed the cold waters of the river to envelop me in their tentacles. I opened my eyes but couldn't see a thing. The rain had raised the water level and increased the river's flow, which in turn had stirred up the silt from the muddy bed. For some odd reason, I felt at peace there, under the water, my lungs depleted of air. I felt as though I were not buried under fifteen feet of moving water at all but, rather, wrapped in the arms of God. Here was the cleansing I had sought, just like all those years ago when Pastor Flowers had baptized me in these same waters.

Eventually, my lungs ran out of oxygen and began to ache. I flailed my arms wildly, struggling, not only to break the bonds of the dark water, but to free myself from the shackles of my past. The anger, the frustration.

The sorrow. Coming to the surface was like being baptized all over again. I'd not only survived, I'd been reborn. As I treaded water, I turned my face skyward and let the rain wash away all that remained of the gunk that had accumulated on my soul over the years. Whether it was simply the buoyancy of the water or the shedding of so much pain, I don't know, but I felt light enough to keep rising right out of the water and back up to the ledge from which I'd stepped.

Finally, when the water level started to rise and my legs began to numb, I paddled over to the river's edge and climbed out. There was a trail that wound through some brush and stands of serviceberry to where my truck was parked. When I arrived, I found Becky and Lizzy there waiting for me, standing under a large umbrella. Lizzy's face lit up like a million-watt bulb. I didn't miss the smile on Becky's face either. It was the smile I had longed to see. And the fact that it was directed at me ...

I gave in to it.

Without thinking, I ran to them, wrapped them both in my arms, held them against my soaked body. After a few seconds, Lizzy turned her face up and said, "We're gonna be okay, aren't we, Daddy."

I smiled at her. "Yes, baby girl. We're going to be okay."

CHAPTER 29

WHEN I ARRIVED BACK at the hospital, I headed straight for my dad's ICU room. Mom was there, seated beside his bed, and Tom was there too. He greeted me with a much-needed bear hug and gave me his chair. Dad was awake and smiled when I sat down. I took his hand and looked into his eyes, finding what I was looking for. There was peace in them. But there was also sorrow. I opened my mouth to speak but he stopped me.

"Ah ... no."

My mom squeezed his other hand. "What is it, Walter?"

Dad stared me straight in the eyes. "I ... uh." He paused. His voice was hoarse and I could tell his throat was sore by the way he winced when he swallowed. "I ... never, no." Again, he paused, swallowed, furrowed his brow. He was concentrating intensely on what he wanted to say. He needed to get this right. "I ... s-sorry." He put his head back on his pillow and sighed.

Mom started crying. Tom put a hand on my shoulder. They both knew those were the two words my dad needed to say and I needed to hear. He was sorry. Sorry for all the torment, for the harsh words, for the negligence, for the condescension. He was sorry for making life with him a hell.

Tears pooled in my eyes and a lump so big I thought I'd choke on it formed in my throat. I turned my head and found Becky and Lizzy standing in the doorway of the room and I was glad they were both there to hear this exchange, especially Lizzy. She needed to hear this too.

Turning back to my dad, I dashed a tear from my eye and said,

"Dad, I forgive you. I do. It's done now. Okay? Let's put it all behind us."

Tom squeezed my shoulder and whispered an amen. Mom put her head on my dad's arm and sobbed quietly. Behind me, Lizzy approached and rested her head on my shoulder. Becky wrapped an arm around my chest and gave me a gentle hug. What I had said seemed simple, just a few words, a few sentences, but the impact it had on my soul was colossal. I was free. I was finally totally free.

Dad smiled as tears rolled from his eyes and tracked down his cheeks. He was a changed man. I saw that now. We were all changed. The old had passed away and things were made new.

Finally, Dad patted my hand to get my attention. He swallowed again and winced. Pulling his hand from mine he looked around at all the tubing and machines and monitors and tapped his chest. "I ... uh, big. No." He shook his head, looked at my mom. "I ... uh."

"He wants to thank you for changing his life," my mom said.

Dad glanced at her. "No. Yes."

Then back to me he patted his chest again. "I ... big."

"He wants to say he's proud of you, Dad," Lizzy said.

Dad smiled big at Lizzy and nodded. "Yes!"

Now it was my time to bawl. The gates lifted and the tears came and I did nothing to hold them back. I needed a good cry.

***

Two days later Lizzy and I were settling into an apartment. My parents' home had been gutted by the fire. It had burned fast and by the time I'd gotten my dad out and the fire trucks arrived it was too late. Nothing could be salvaged. They would rebuild with the insurance money and my mom offered to have an in-law quarters added where she and Dad could reside while Lizzy and I lived in the main house. It was a nice gesture but I refused. It was time for Lizzy and me to make it on our own. Tom had managed to sell our home back in Pennsylvania so we'd take that money and find a house nearby and fix it up.

Becky and Mom helped us move what little furniture we had into the apartment. Tom stayed a couple extra days to help as well. When we were finished and the table and chairs were in place, the sofa parked against the wall, and television hooked up I wandered outside to get some fresh air. Winter had returned to the region and the air was brisk and cool. Behind the apartment building there was a wood and a trail that wound to a nearby park. With my hands in my pockets, I headed for the trail. Lizzy was busy helping the others unpack our new plates and glasses and stock the refrigerator. But I needed a few moments alone.

Before I hit the tree line I heard a voice call my name. It was Becky.

I turned and found her running across the apartment building's back lawn. When she reached me, she was slightly out of breath and her nose was red. She wore a heavy sweater and wool cap.

"Hey, mind if I join you?"

"Not at all. I was just going to take a little walk."

"Collect your thoughts?"

I nodded. "Something like that."

"Is it strange?"

"Is what strange?"

"Moving in here, leaving the familiar and starting over."

I looked at her and smiled. "There're still some familiar things around. But no, it's not as strange as I thought it would be."

"You've come a long way."

"Both of us have. Lizzy and me."

"She's so strong."

"She's so much like her mother."

Becky glanced at me. "And her father."

There was a moment of silence between us while we walked. The woods was mostly noiseless. Only the occasional high-pitched chirping of a chickadee broke the silence. Finally, Becky said, "And where do I fit into this starting over you and Lizzy are doing?"

"I hope you'll be here," I said. "I hope you'll be part of our lives." I wanted to tell her more but wasn't sure how she'd respond. My feelings for Becky had grown and blossomed to more than just a sister-in-law or friend.

She slowed her walking. "You mean part of your lives as the aunt that hangs out occasionally or …"

I stopped and faced her. The look in her brown eyes told me I didn't have anything to worry about. "Part of our lives in a more permanent way."

"I can't be Annie," she said.

"You're not Annie."

"I can't replace her, though."

"I don't want you to."

"Can you love me for me and not because I remind you of her?"

I took both her hands in mine. "I already do."

Then I leaned forward and put my lips to hers, nothing passionate, just a gentle kiss.

CHAPTER 30

A MONTH HAD PASSED AND Lizzy and I had bought a house not a mile from my parents' home. It was a nice place, three bedrooms, two floors, reminded both of us of our house back in Pennsylvania. It needed work, though. The previous owners were the original occupants dating all the way back to the early 1950s. And not much had changed. Worn carpeting covered most of the wood flooring; outdated and faded floral wallpaper hid the walls.

I'd been spending more and more time with Becky, which Lizzy fully approved of, and Becky had been spending more and more time helping us give the house a facelift. On the first day of scraping wallpaper, Becky and Lizzy manned the steamer and I came behind them and scraped off the wet paper. Some of it came right off in big, soggy chunks, but most had to be worked at. Midway across the first wall in the living room, I stopped and sat on the floor, legs crossed.

Becky turned off the steamer and cocked her head to one side. "You tired already?"

I shook my head. "Nope." Scraping that wallpaper had suddenly reminded me of the conversation I'd had with Tom on the porch of my parents' house the night before Thanksgiving. He'd urged me to forgive my dad and I'd told him it wasn't that easy. Getting rid of life's hurts and pains wasn't as simple as slapping new wallpaper over the old stuff. The old stuff had to be removed first so the new paper could be placed on a clean surface. Six months after Annie's death, I was finally ready to peel off that old paper and allow God to prepare my heart for some new stuff.

Becky sat on the floor next to me and Lizzy took the other side.

She was walking now with no assistive device and barely showed a limp. Her recovery had been remarkable.

"What is it then?" Becky asked.

"Yeah, Dad," Lizzy said. "What gives?"

"What gives?" I ruffled her hair. "Where'd you hear that?"

She shrugged. "I don't know."

"You gooney bird," I said and kissed her on the forehead.

Lizzy looked around the room, then turned to me. "Dad, are we home?"

Once again, my seven-year-old daughter had blown me away with her insight.

I knew what she meant, that she asked about more than just geography, and I realized at that moment how far we had come. But home was something I never expected to find again.

I still thought about Annie all the time, and missed her terribly. But I was also happy a lot. More each day, it seemed.

But was I home?

I put my arm around Lizzy and the other around Becky. Becky rested her head on my shoulder and it felt good.

I felt good.

I smiled. "Yes, baby girl, we're home now."

We'd gone a million miles to get there, but we were finally home again.

Made in the USA
Las Vegas, NV
10 June 2022

50077701R00132